## Credits

Thanks to Allison from Allison Leslie Editing & Coaching who edits
my books and puts up with my idiosyncratic style. My wife who is
so supportive and believed in me. Last my dogs who watch me act
out the fight scenes and must wonder what the hell has gotten into
their boss.

THANK YOU FOR READING!

I hope you enjoy reading this book as much as I enjoyed writing it. Reviews are so helpful to authors. I really appreciate all reviews, both positive and negative. If you want to leave one, you can do so on Amazon, through the website or Twitter.


About the Author

Christopher C Tubbs is a descendent of a long line of Dorset clay miners and has chased his family tree back to the 16th century in the Isle of Purbeck. He has been a public speaker at conferences for most of his career in the Aerospace and Automotive industries and was one of the founders of a successful games company back in the 1990's. Now in his sixties he finally got around to writing the stories he has been dreaming about for years. He lives in the Netherlands Antilles with his wife, two Dutch Shepherds and Norwegian Forest cats.

You can visit him on his website
www.thedorsetboy.com
Or tweet him @ChristopherCTu3

# The Dorset Boy Series Timeline

**1792 – 1795**   Book 1: A Talent for Trouble
Marty joins the Navy as an Assistant Steward and ends up a midshipman.

**1795 – 1798**   Book 2: The Special Operations Flotilla
Marty is a founder member of the Special Operations Flotilla, learns to be a spy and passes as lieutenant.

**1799 – 1802**   Book 3: Agent Provocateur
Marty teams up with Linette to infiltrate Paris, marries Caroline, becomes a father and fights pirates in Madagascar.

**1802 – 1804**   Book 4: In Dangerous Company
Marty and Caroline are in India helping out Arthur Wellesley, combating French efforts to disrupt the East India Company and French sponsored pirates on Reunion. James Stockley born

**1804 – 1805**   Book 5: The Tempest
Piracy in the Caribbean, French interference, Spanish gold and the death of Nelson. Marty makes Captain.

**1806 – 1807**   Book 6: Vendetta

A favour carried out for a prince, a new ship, the S.O.F. move to Gibraltar, the battle of Maida, counter espionage in Malta and a Vendetta declared and closed.

**1807 – 1809**   Book 7: The Trojan Horse

Rescue of the Portuguese royal family, Battle of the Basque Roads with Thomas Cochrane, and back to the Indian Ocean and another conflict with the French Intelligence Service.

**1809 – 1811**   Book 8: La Licorne

Marty takes on the role of Viscount Wellington's Head of Intelligence. Battle of The Lines of Torres Vedras, siege of Cadiz, skulduggery, espionage and blowing stuff up to confound the French.

**1813 – 1814**   Book 10: Silverthorn

The prince finally gets his way and Marty is made a Viscount and promoted to Commodore but there is a price as he is back to the Caribbean as Governor of Aruba. That of course is a front as his real mission is to ferment rebellion in South America. Then back to Europe and the abdication of Napoleon and his exile to Elba.

**1815-1816**    Book 11: Exile

After 100 days in exile Napoleon returns to France and Marty tries to hunt him down. After the battle of Waterloo Marty again escorts him into Exile on St Helena. His help is requested by the Governor of Ceylon against the rebels in Kandy.

**1817-1818**    Book 12: Dynasty

To Paris to stop an assassination, then the Mediterranean to further British interests in the region. Finally, to Calcutta as Military Attaché to take part in the war with the Maratha Empire. Beth comes into her own as a spy, but James prefers the Navy life.

**1818-1819**    Book 13: Empire

The end of the third Anglo-Maratha war and the establishment of the Raj. Intrigue in India, war with the Pindaris, the foundation of Singapore. Shipwreck, sea war and storms.

# Contents

CHAPTER 1: READING IN

CHAPTER 2: A CHANGE OF IDENTITY

CHAPTER 3: AMBUSH

CHAPTER 4: BETRAYAL

CHAPTER 5: VENGEANCE IS MINE

CHAPTER 6: INSERTION

CHAPTER 7: PARIS

CHAPTER 8: THE BEST INTENTIONS

CHAPTER 9: RUMBLED

CHAPTER 10: A BRIEF RESPITE

CHAPTER 11: SURPRISE SURPRISE!

CHAPTER 12: CROSSING THE LINE

CHAPTER 13: THE MADAGASCAR CAPER

CHAPTER 14: FINISHING UP

CHAPTER 15: HOMEWARD BOUND.

CHAPTER 16: INTO INSANITY

CHAPTER 17: A PASSAGE TO INDIA

CHAPTER 18: STORMED

CHAPTER 19: SLEIGHT OF HAND

CHAPTER 20: EVERY CLOUD . . .

EPILOGUE

AUTHOR'S NOTE

AN EXCERPT FROM BOOK 4: IN DANGEROUS COMPANY

# Chapter 1: Reading In

Newly commissioned Lieutenant Martin Stockley stood in front of a long mirror in his room at the headquarters of the Special Operations Flotilla, or The Farm as they called it, and admired the fit of the new uniform that had just arrived from his tailor in London. He was trying to decide whether to wear his silver buckled shoes or hessian boots when there was a knock on the door.

"Come in," he called.

Will Barbour, their steward, entered and said,

"Oh Sir, you do look proper good. Suits you to a tee. Mr. Armand said if you could hurry up as they is all waiting on yer."

*Shoes it is then,* Marty concluded and pulled on one of his three new pairs. The men had asked if they could celebrate his promotion with a dinner and 'a few wets', which meant they were in for a wild time this evening. Sailors seldom did just 'a few wets' and had a prodigious capacity for alcohol.

The Deal smugglers were ready to supply the best brandy and wines to them for free, as the S.O.F. were their protection and the source of most of their wealth. Bill, their leader, and his lieutenants had been invited as well. This evening would be long, merry, and test the stamina of the strongest.

Marty entered the large dining room to a roar of congratulation. He made a show of acknowledging the cheers then struck a pose. He waited until they quieted.

"Thank you, thank you, thank you," he said to the left, centre, and right in turn as he looked around the room, registering the faces.

"I understand that Monsieur du Dumaine has taken over the kitchens for this celebration, so I am sure we will all eat well!"

Another cheer!

*This would not go down well at the Admiralty!* He thought, and he was right. The Admiralty would have a very dim view of the familiarity between the men and officers. But this was the S.O.F. and things worked differently here.

Let them enjoy themselves, he thought, I will break the bad news about the next mission later.

The next morning, despite hangovers, they ordered the Lark and Alouette to be prepared for a six-week voyage. They would go hunting neutral ships supplying goods to the French in opposition to any agreements their governments may have with the British.

Marty left for the dock to check on progress and to read himself in as the Lark's official commander. He was dressed in his best uniform and hat and wore the dress sword that the love of his life, Lady Caroline Candor, had given him. As he walked up to the dock, he thought it ironic that his cutter, and the sloop moored next to her, shared the same name in two languages at times. But this morning, the Alouette was called the Swan as she was in English waters.

It was a fine morning, although very cold, and he enjoyed the short walk from The Farm to the dock on the river Stour where their three craft were moored. He soon warmed up, and his breath steamed. Blaez, his young Dutch Shepherd dog, trotted along with him checking out the verges for any trace of either intruding dogs or receptive bitches and marking his territory at regular intervals.

He arrived at the dock to find it a hive of activity. Wagons were lined up, ready to unload food and other dry stores into nets which were hoisted aboard and down into the hold. This was faster and needed less men than forming chain gangs. Water barrels were being loaded into empty wagons to be filled from a spring a short ride away as the river water was brackish this close to the sea.

He didn't notice the elegant coach tucked away behind one of the storage sheds as he only had eyes for his ship.

He walked up the gang plank on to the deck of the Cutter that was his first command as a lieutenant. She was a little beauty with her long, elegant bowsprit, which was almost half as long as her hull and single mast. She was normally gaff-rigged with multiple fore sails that gave her fantastic manoeuvrability but could carry a couple of square sails if she needed to swim downwind as well.

She was armed with ten twenty-four-pound carronades, which gave her a close in punch that was far heavier than anyone would expect. When she fought in consort with the Alouette, they could give a nasty surprise to anyone who took them on. The carronades had the advantage that they only needed four men each to man them, or three in a pinch. But their short range could put you in trouble if up against guns with longer range.

The men smiled at him as he made his way aft to the wheel, and Blaez greeted many of them with a headbutt and a lick. When he got to Tom, he reared up on his hind legs and planted them on his chest. Looked him straight in the eye, and licked him from the base of his neck to the tip of his chin. Marty laughed at that and from the soppy look on Tom's face.

He beckoned Midshipman Campbell over and asked him to assemble the men on the main deck. When they had settled, he took out his commission and started to read.

"By the Commissioners for executing the Office of the Lord High Admiral of Great Britain &c and of all His Majesty's Plantations &c.

To Lieut. Martin Alfred Stockley, hereby appointed Master and Commander of His Majesty's Ship, Snipe.

By virtue of the Power and Authority to us given, We do hereby constitute and appoint you Master and Commander of His Majesties Ship, Snipe, willing and requiring you forthwith to go on board and take upon you the Charge and Command of Master and Commander in her accordingly. Strictly Charging and Commanding all the Officers and Company belonging to the said ship subordinate to you to behave themselves jointly and severally in their respective Employments with all the Respect and Obedience unto you, their said Master and Commander; And you, likewise, to observe and execute as well, the General printed Instructions as what Orders and Directions you shall from time to time receive from your superior Officers for His Majesty's service. Hereof, nor you nor any of you may fail, as you will answer the contrary at your peril. And for so doing this, shall be your Warrant. Given under our hands and the Seal of the Office Admiralty, this 20th day of September in the one thousandth seven hundredth and ninety eighth Year of His Majesty's Reign.

By Command of their Lordships"

He reached the end and looked up. He was faced with a sea of smiling but expectant faces.

*Oh, shit they want me to make a speech!* He thought in panic. His brain went into fast mode like he was in combat.

"Looking around all your faces," he swept his gaze over the men and stopped in astonishment. There dressed as a common sailor was, Caroline?

He coughed to cover the gap.

"I see many who have sailed and fought with me in the past and some new ones."

He pointedly didn't look at Caroline.

"Well, you old hands can tell the new hands what to expect. But one thing I will tell all of you is that you can all expect to continue doing the jobs that no one else wants, in ways no one else will. We are the S.O.F. We will bring pain and confusion to the French and anyone who sides with them." He paused to look around again.

"And if we are lucky, make a few bob for ourselves," he concluded, causing a chuckle.

He raised his hat to the men and stepped back, signifying he had finished.

The deck erupted in cheers when someone who sounded very much like John Smith called, "Three cheers and a tiger for the skipper!"

Marty waited until the cheers died down then said, "Right, now get back to work, you idle lubbers. There is no excuse to be shirking!"

To Tom he said,

"And I want to see the sailor with the auburn hair and green eyes in my cabin as soon as you can find her."

There was no marine on duty outside his cabin as everyone was busy with the provisioning. So, there was no announcement. The door opened and in walked Caroline dressed in sailor's slops with her hair hidden under a woollen hat.

"The hat's not right. No Navy man would wear one of those," he said.

"I'll have to remember that when I stow away next time," she said and pulled it off, allowing her lustrous wavy hair to tumble over her shoulders.

"I didn't want to miss you reading yourself in but didn't want to distract you. You were very commanding."

"Who gave you the slops?" he asked.

"If I told you, I would have to kill you," she said and moved in closer.

"I see. I will have to torture you for the information," he laughed.

"Ooh, I can't wait!" she purred and moved in for a kiss.

"Well, my little kitten," he said and kissed her on the nose, "you will have to. We can't be making that kind of noise here as the whole crew would be able to hear."

"You could always gag me," she teased.

Marty turned her around and gave her a whack on the backside as he pushed her towards the door.

"Get thee behind me, devil woman," he growled as the thought tempted him.

"That sounds interesting," she replied, giving him her best sultry look over her shoulder.

"I'll see you in a couple of hours at The Farm. I have a ship to get ready," he said firmly and pushed her out the door.

"Don't forget the gag!" she called as she left.


Tom came in almost immediately with Midshipman Campbell.

"Gag?" he said with raised eyebrows and a twinkle in his eye.

"Don't ask," said Marty and sat at his desk.

He then looked at Campbell and said, "And you can wipe that smirk off your face if you don't want to spend the next week scrubbing the bilges."

Campbell managed, to his credit, to put on a straight face.

"You have something to report?" Marty asked him.

"Oh yes. I mean, aye aye, sir," he stammered.

"Mr. Campbell, if I have to wring every report out of you, this is going to be a very long voyage for both of us," Marty cautioned.

"Aye aye, sir! I wish to report, that we will be finished loading food in the next hour and water by sunset."

Marty looked at Tom, who was leant against the door frame, and raised an eyebrow in query. Tom gave a slight nod. Marty gave his attention back to Campbell.

"We will sail tomorrow morning on the ebb tide. Let the men have a last evening in town. I want them all back on board by midnight. Anyone who isn't, will be docked a week's pay and rum ration. Make sure they know it."

"Aye, sir."

There was a muffled cheer from outside. Marty looked up at the open skylight.

"They probably know already, but we need to maintain some kind of chain of command," he concluded.

"Now, do you have all the store reports?"

"Aye, sir," Campbell replied and handed over a sheaf of papers which he pulled from his pocket.

Marty sighed as he saw that he would spend the next couple of hours doing the bookwork.

The problem with cutters is they don't warrant a purser, he thought.


Three hours later, he got back to The Farm. Caroline was reading a book in the common room while she waited for him. She put it down and rose to greet him with an extended kiss. Once they finished, he grinned and said,

"What's for dinner? I'm famished!"

"Will has prepared some fresh sole in white wine and butter sauce. He got the recipe from Roland," she replied.

"Wonderful! What are you reading?" he asked and picked up her book. "The Abbess, by William Henry Ireland," he read off the cover. "That's supposed to be practically pornographic, isn't it? If your chaplain catches you with that, you will be excommunicated!"

Caroline laughed, gave him a wicked look, and replied archly,

"Well, I thought it might give me some ideas."

"Well, they can wait until after dinner," he said as Will knocked on the door to announce that it was ready.

They retired to bed early and as they were the only ones there, it didn't matter how much noise they made, and the gag wasn't really needed. Although it did get tried… At least once.

# Chapter 2: A Change of Identity

They were just getting ready to cast off the next morning when a rider galloped up to the dock and dismounted as soon as his horse came to a stop. The horse was covered in sweat and looked to have been ridden hard. He hailed the Lark and waved his messenger bag at the quarterdeck, obviously relieved to have caught them before they left.

The gangplank had just been pulled in, so Marty jumped from the deck to the dock and walked over to meet him.

"I'm glad I made it in time, sir," the messenger said. "I have an urgent change of orders for you from The Admiralty. I will need a confirmation that you have read and understood them."

Marty took the package, broke the seal, scanned the contents, and signed the proffered receipt.

"Walk that horse over to that farm," he said and pointed him in the right direction, "Change him for one of ours if you need to get back immediately. Tell the marine that I said it was OK. Make sure you get some food and drink before you leave."

He then walked down the dock to the Alouette.

"Armand!" He called, and Armand came to the rail "A change of plans. You are on your own. I'm ordered to go and annoy the Dutch!"

"Pourquoi?" Armand replied.

"Can't say," Marty said, looking around as if he was looking for eavesdroppers.

"Oh, one of those," Armand said with a grin, "Well, good hunting and be careful."

"You too!" Marty grinned back.

They set sail on the ebbtide as planned and headed out into the channel. The Alouette headed for their hunting grounds between Roscoff and Brest, that being the most likely place they would find American blockade runners, and the Lark headed Northeast towards the coast of the Batavian Republic.

Marty sat in his cabin in his one comfy chair and re-read his orders. Apparently, Jeroen, the agent he had worked with the last time he was there, had sent a message that there was a regular trade in flax running from Rotterdam down the coast to Calais. Within those cargos was hidden the tax revenue that the French were collecting as a war indemnity. The French figured that a cargo of such little value as flax wouldn't attract attention from prize hungry English captains.

His mission was to disrupt that trade and to capture as prizes, or burn, any ships he could. *A tough call if there is anything bigger than a flipping sloop as escort,* he thought. He was to do it under a guise so they wouldn't make the connection with an internal leak and the British Government. The orders didn't say what nationality he should adopt.

He thought about it for a while as he sat scratching Blaez's ears. An independent with obscure origins, given that he had a mixed crew, would work. He could drop hints about having stolen the cutter and put a false name on the stern. Yes, the more he thought about it, the better it started to sound to him.

"Call for midshipman Campbell, please," he yelled up at the skylight. Two minutes later, Campbell entered after knocking on the door.

"Yes Sir?" he asked, patting the dog on the head as it sniffed him in greeting.

"I want a new name on the stern; the Louise, I think. Paint it to be hard to read, and make it look as old as the rest of the ship. Then get everybody into their privateer outfits and muss the ship up to look like she is privately owned. The crew know what to do, just tell them to do it."

"Aah sir, do I need to dress up as well?" Campbell asked.

"Well, you will bloody well stick out like a spare prick at a floozy's wedding if you don't," Marty responded with more than a trace of irritation.

"This is one of those moments the Admiral mentioned, isn't it? Where things aren't what they seem?" Campbell asked, looking abashed. Marty relented.

"Yes, Mr. Campbell, it is, and for the record, from now on while we are 'in character,' you refer to me as Skipper, and ask the men, not order them. This isn't the Navy anymore," Marty replied, thinking he couldn't expect Campbell to have done anything like this before.

"Sit down for a minute and let me explain."

Campbell sat on the bench by the stern windows.

"We have been ordered to find and either capture or destroy Dutch ships that are carrying bullion to pay the French their war tax. The information came from a trusted source within the Dutch government who took a huge risk to get us the information and must be protected. So, we don't want the Navy to be seen doing this as that would point to the British government having someone on the inside," Marty explained.

"Oh, so we pose as a privateer to cover up the fact we are really Navy!" Campbell exclaimed.

"Yes, so find yourself a pirate costume and practice talking like a common sailor as you aren't Midshipman Campbell anymore but First Mate Campbell. Understood?"

"Aye aye, sir!"

Marty raised an eyebrow.

"Oh, I mean yes, skipper!"

Marty smiled and said, "Better. Just keep practicing that. Off you go."

Campbell stood and was about to salute when he saw the raised eyebrow again and stopped about halfway up. He grinned and turned to leave.

"By the way," Marty said, stopping him in his tracks. "If you have any ideas about how to make the Louise look less British than the Lark, feel free to put them forward."

"Aye, I mean yes, skipper," he said as he left.

After the door closed, Marty grinned to himself and thought, It's a start! But then he had a thought, *Why would they take the risk of sending the tax by ship through hostile waters when they could safely send it by land?* That was troubling and he thought through the possible reasons. *What if someone was setting Jeroen up? What if Jeroen had been caught and they were sending fake messages to try and see if the network actually existed?*

He went up on deck to check on the progress that was being made and was mildly surprised at the change that had come over his ship. Campbell was supervising the removal of the yards on the mast that were used for setting square sails. He also had a couple of men altering the apparent cut of the sails by folding and stitching seams along the edges.

"Well, Mr. Campbell, I can understand the bringing down of the yards, but please explain what the men are doing to my sails," Marty barked.

"Och ay, Skipper," Campbell replied in a broad Scottish accent, causing Marty to raise both eyebrows in surprise. "We be making them look like Swedish cut sails."

"You have experience of Swedish sails?" Marty asked.

"Och ay. I spent six months in Malmo on me last ship and sailed a Swedish cutter for fun."

"Well, they better work as well as ours or you will be unstitching them yourself," Marty joked and slapped him on the back. "And you can drop the Scottish accent until we board a prize."

Tom, Marty's coxswain, and Matai were working on a new name board. They had painted Louise in dark blue on a red background, which Marty found hard to read in itself. Now, they were bashing it with chains to make it look aged, which obscured some letters even more.

Tom got one end and Matai the other, and held it up for Marty to inspect.

"That is bloody perfect," he said in honest admiration. "Let's get it mounted."

He looked around and if it wasn't for the carronades, she could be from anywhere. *The carronades!* he thought, *how can we disguise them?* He waited for Tom to return and then called him and John Smith (his quartermaster) to him.

"We need to do something to disguise the carronades," he said, "Any ideas?"

"It's the slides and that great, gaping, gob of a barrel that gives them away," said John.

"Yes, they look nothing like six or even nine pounders, do they?" Added Marty, "I think we need to keep them covered and mount as many swivels along the sides as we can. We will need to get in close and board if we are to make any money. If we need the carronades, it will be as a last resort anyway."

With nothing else to do, he had a game of tug with Blaez then went to the charts to check on their position. Satisfied, he gave the order for a change of course toward Calais.

# Chapter 3: Ambush

They made their way up the French coast looking for any Batavian merchant ships heading the other way. They stopped and took a couple of French coasters to help bulk up their cover story, but they were unexciting and only provided some fresh stores and a barrico or two of cheap wine.

They took their time and looked in every cove and estuary as they went in case their prey was hiding during daylight hours. They reached the Northern tip of France and Marty decided to 'hang around' there rather than go up past Antwerp. They reduced sail to the minimum overnight and resumed their search at false dawn the next morning.

By lunchtime, they hadn't seen anything. Marty wondered if anything had passed then in the dark, so he headed back to Calais under full sail.

Again nothing, and reversed course to try again. With nothing else to do, Marty started weapons training to keep the men occupied.

He donned his weapons harness and went to find Campbell. It was time to assess his capabilities. Blaez was curious and followed him on deck.

"Mr. Campbell!" He called and the mid turned from watching some of the men going at it with wooden cutlasses and walked over to him.

"I heard you were a fist fighter, but can you use a blade?" Marty asked

Campbell ran his eyes over Marty's weapons rig noting the hanger, fighting knife, and pair of double-barrelled pistols. He then looked down at the hessian boots Marty wore and noted that there was an additional knife in each of them.

"I feel underdressed, Skipper," he said with a smile.

"Oh, this little set up?" grinned Marty, "It's all the rage for us pirates, you know."

"Wooden blades?" He asked hopefully.

Marty drew his hanger and said,

"I think steel is much more of a test, don't you?"

"May I get my sword from my cabin?" Campbell asked, putting a bold face on it.

"Of course," Marty replied and bowed him away with a flourish.

Campbell returned with what looked like a cavalry sabre on his waist. *Heavy that,* Marty observed and when it was drawn, he could see it was both longer and heavier than his hanger with a curved blade designed for chopping. It had a point, so it could be thrust as well, if needed, but that would be awkward.

Marty assumed his customary knife fighter's stance, and Campbell took up his guard in preparation. They circled, assessing each other. Campbell swung first. A scything slash to the midriff, which Marty avoided by stepping back and letting it pass. He noted that Campbell didn't have any trouble controlling the blade at the end of the swing and used the momentum to bring it back to guard. Suddenly Blaez came out of nowhere snarling viciously and hit Campbell high in the chest with his front paws, knocking him flat on his back. Campbell found himself looking straight into the eyes of what looked like a very angry wolf. The dog was stood on his chest with his nose inches from his and his lips drawn back in a snarl.

Marty rushed in, grabbed Blaez by the scruff, and speaking softly, eased him off the shocked and frightened mid. He beckoned Tom over and asked him to lock the dog in his cabin after he had praised him and given him a good neck scratch to let him know he wasn't angry at him.

Campbell got to his feet.

"Sorry about that," said Marty, "I think he thought you were really attacking me. He's never seen me practice before. Are you alright?"

"I'm fine, apart from a bruised behind. Damn, he was fast. I didn't even see him coming! He will be deuced handy in a fight."

They both laughed at that, and Marty noticed that all the men had stopped practicing to watch. He inclined his head towards them and said,

"Shall we continue? The boys look as if they want a show."

They took up their guard positions again and resumed a slow circling anticlockwise. Marty suddenly reversed direction and simultaneously launched a high attack, forcing Campbell to parry and then reversed the swing to cut low at his thigh. Campbell skipped back out of range and took up his guard again.

Marty grinned, and they both advanced swinging and parrying, setting up a clamour of crashing steel. It stopped suddenly as they came together, blade to blade, and Campbell felt the point of the fighting knife pressed against his side.

"You're dead," said Marty.

"The knife?" asked Campbell, not moving even a fraction of an inch.

"Yup. Don't get in close if the other man has one. Lesson learnt?"

Campbell nodded and as they stepped apart, bowed and saluted with his sword.

"You have a good sword arm, but that cleaver is heavy and if the fight goes on for too long, will wear you out," cautioned Marty, "So either sw…"

"SAIL HO! COMING FROM ASTERN FAST," yelled the lookout, stopping Marty mid-word.

Marty sheathed his blades and raced to the quarterdeck to get a telescope. He stood on a carronade to get some height. He could see that whatever it was had a gaff rig and was carrying all the sail she could.

"Make all sail," he commanded, and the men ran to obey.

"ANOTHER SAIL. DEAD AHEAD AND COMING RIGHT AT US," cried the lookout again.

"What the hell! Mr. Campbell, get up there and check them both out."

"THEY BE BOTH FRENCH!" reported Campbell in a voice that could have been heard half a mile away.

"Beat to quarters!" Marty ordered as Campbell slid down a stay to the deck.

"Two French luggers, sir. The forward one is steering to cut us off. The one astern is closing fast and has the weather gage on us."

Marty knew that French luggers carried up to fourteen nine-pounders and had a significant punch.

"I knew this was too good to be true," he cried, "It's a fucking trap!"

"DECK THERE. A THIRD SAIL TO LARBOARD. SAME TYPE AND IS CLOSING."

"Trying to box us in," Campbell noted.

"WHICH IS GOING TO GET TO US FIRST?" yelled Marty to the lookout.

"THE ONE FORRAD OF US," came the reply.

Marty turned to Campbell and saw Tom and John Smith close by.

"Mr. Campbell, I would be obliged if you would get the carronades loaded on both sides. Chain and Langridge larboard side and Ball Starboard!"

Campbell went straight to work yelling orders to the gun crews. They were overmanned by the measure of the Navy but just right for a privateer, so they could easily fight both sides if they needed to.

"John, I want you on the wheel. Get an extra man to help you."

Marty ran to the foredeck and looked long and hard at the lugger approaching from in front. He then looked at the other two, calculating closing speeds and angles in his head.

"John! Steer straight for him," he ordered as he got back to the wheel, pointing at the forward lugger.

Marty saw that their target was heeled over with the wind on his starboard side. If he could pass him on his larboard side, it would restrict his gunnery even if it gave away the wind gauge. It would also give his carronades an easier shot at his rigging and deck.

"Mr. Campbell, I will steer straight for him. I don't think he is fitted with bow chasers, but if he jinks, expect some incoming. Bow on, we are a small target. When we are one and a half cables from him, I will veer to starboard, and you can let him have it with the Larboard battery. I want that gun," and he pointed at the foremost carronade, "to go for his quarterdeck. The rest, take down his rigging. We will then wear to starboard and as we pass him again; we will serve him with the other battery into his hull. After that, we will go head-to-head with that ship astern of us."

*This is going to be really close. I won't have more than a few minutes to get sorted if we get damaged and I want to get on that second bastard's starboard side so he will shield me from the third,* Marty thought.

Marty knew he had to use the advantage given by his carronades. Their smashing power would help even the odds, but he had to get in close enough! The last thing he needed was a long-range slugging match.

The range to the forward lugger was closing rapidly. Marty saw the twitch of their sails just before he jinked to starboard and loosed off a broadside at about half a mile.

"Hold fast, boys!" Marty shouted to encourage his men. "Them Frenchies can't hit a cow's arse with a paddle," he taunted.

The range closed fast, and he held his nerve until they were easily less than one and a half cables apart. The French didn't have a single gun run out! He had beaten them to it! He slashed his right arm down to signal John Smith to go to starboard, and he watched the French ship as they started to pass down her side.

Campbell held his fire until they were almost broadside to broadside. Four of the carronades coughed as one, followed a couple of seconds later by the forward one. The effect on the other ship was devastating. The mast took at least a couple of direct hits, and the rigging was shredded. The mast shuddered and snapped off about halfway up. As they passed her stern, he could see no-one on her quarterdeck. Whoever aimed that forward gun had done a good job.

He commanded them to wear, and they swung through the wind to reverse their course. It took only a few minutes to come up on the stricken ship and he was about to order the starboard guns to fire, when her flag fall to the deck.

"They've struck!" called Campbell.

Marty ignored them and turned his attention to the second ship that he was now going head-to-head with. He took the time to look to starboard and check on the seaward vessel. She was closing but not fast enough to get to them before they met the other.

Marty knew that if the other captain had been watching, he would expect Marty to try the same tactic again. So, he had to think up something else bloody quickly.

He looked up at the pennant and at the tell tails on the sails. The wind was coming from their forward starboard quarter, and they were steering as close into it as they could. He had an idea. It would be dangerous, daring, and could go horribly wrong, but if it worked, he would throw the Frenchman into confusion.

He ordered John to drop them off a point so it would look like they would try and pass down the starboard side of their adversary. Then he told the men to prepare to tack to starboard on his command. He had the larboard carronades loaded with a double load of ball but not rolled out. That made them into monstrous sawn-off shotguns with twelve 4 Lb balls per gun. The crews were to aim for the enemy's bow. This would test their gunnery to the limit.

They raced closer.

Half a mile apart.

The enemy ran his starboard guns out. That part was working.

He waited.

Six hundred yards.

Four Hundred Yards.

"Roll out!" He ordered.

"Skipper?" Prompted John Smith.

Marty ignored him.

Two hundred.

One hundred and fifty and,

"Hard to Starboard! Tack the ship! Fire as you bear!"

He kept his eyes on the other ship and as they swung across her bow... Had he left it too late? Their bowsprit looked like a spear heading straight for their Larboard side!

The guns coughed their deadly loads one after the other. The enemy ship seemed to shake from end to end and her bow seemed to cave in on itself. Then her head started to swing around as her captain instinctively tried to avoid a collision that would sink them both.

After that, the Lark's sails grabbed the wind and she shot forward as the Frenchman passed her stern. Marty braced as he half expected the French to rake him but only one gun fired and hit their transom.

Marty heard furious barking coming from his cabin as Blaez swore at the intruder. Seconds later, there was a crash and he appeared on the deck with the hair from the back of his head to his tail standing on end making him look twice as big and one angry dog. He jumped up and put his front paws on the rail and barked furiously at the other ship.

The men cheered him.

Their opponent had almost come to a stop and was noticeably down by the bow, so Marty turned his attention to the third one.

"SHIT! EVERYONE DOWN!" he shouted and grabbing Blaez, threw himself to the deck with the dog beside him.

The third lugger had closed and had swung broadside on about three cables away. Her guns flashed as her broadside rippled down her deck and chain and bar shot howled overhead ripping the mainsail from top to bottom and taking several large chunks out of the mast.

"Larboard battery is ready, sir," shouted Campbell as Marty got to his feet.

*Bugger this,* he thought.

"We will close and give her one broadside and then board her. So, make it a good one! Marines, are you ready?" There was a loud cheer!

"Boarders, are you ready?" An even louder cheer.

"LET'S DO THIS!" He shouted.

They steered for the French to get them alongside at close pistol shot. He checked his weapons and told Blaez to sit beside him. He could see the French frantically trying to reload.

Ten yards separated them, and the French guns were being rolled out when he shouted, "FIRE". At that range, the carronades were devastating, and the side of the lugger was peppered with star shaped holes. They ground up beside her and he yelled,

"Grapples away!" Then once they were tight,

"Boarders away!" And launched himself over the rail onto the other deck.

He held both his pistols and shot one man in the chest as he stood up from behind a cannon and another in the face as he rushed at him sword raised. A third to his left was about to spear him with a boarding pike when a brindled shape flew over the side, sank its teeth into his shoulder and dragged him to the floor. Then his men arrived, and he was swept away from his dog and its victim.

The fight was short, nasty, and deadly. No quarter given or asked for. The numbers were about even, but the superior weapons training of the Larks made the difference.

The French surrendered after their captain died when Campbell's sabre almost split him in half. Marty accepted the surrender from a wounded and visibly shocked junior officer then stood back to figure out what to do next.

His eyes popped open in realization and he cried,

"Blaez. Where is Blaez?"

He turned around scanning the deck in panic. He breathed a huge sigh of relief when Blaez wandered up to him with a big doggy grin on his face and blood all around his chops.

Marty knelt down in front of Blaez and put his arm around his shoulders. The dog raised a paw and nuzzled him for Marty to scratch his chest.

"You are a very good boy."

"Aye, I reckon he saved your skin back there," marked Tom Savage from just behind him.

"You saw?" Marty asked.

"Aye, I did. He followed you to the rail and watched you jump over. You shot them two Frenchies and there was a third about to skewer you from the side. He suddenly rushed forward, jumped across using the rail of t'other ship to launch himself at that bloke. By the time I got there, he had him by the throat and had choked the life out of him."

"A regular bloody killer," laughed Marty.

"He'll fit in right well with this lot!" replied Tom.

# Chapter 4: Betrayal

They sent out boats to look for survivors of the second lugger to no avail. It had sunk in the time it took to finish the fight with the third one. It had almost full sail on when its bow was shot away, and it had taken on water so fast that only a few men had survived. Campbell reported that he thought only two of the carronades had scored, but that had been enough.

The first lugger was still drifting a way off. The damage to her rigging was bad enough that the crew knew they could never outrun the agile cutter.

They buried the dead at sea and tended to their wounded. The Larks got off relatively lightly in as much as they had two dead marines who hadn't gotten down fast enough when they took the broadside, four wounded enough to be unfit for duty, and half a dozen with minor wounds. The French had come off a lot worse.

Marty decided that they would send the two prizes back to base, leaving the Lark at sea with a regular crew. He had some unfinished business to attend to. He wanted to know why someone had gone to all this trouble to lay a trap and what was Jeroen's role in it.

He interrogated the remaining officers of the prizes and just got told that they were ordered to look for and intercept a cutter that would be cruising between Antwerp and Calais. They were to bring the captured crew and officers to The Hague and hand them over to the French Embassy.

He got prize crews installed under the command of Midshipman Campbell. The second lugger was commanded by Wilson, the giant senior Topman, who he temporarily rated as a mate. He made sure adequate repairs were made and sent them on their way with a written report to Wickham and Lord Hood.

Meanwhile, he turned his bow to the North with the idea that a short visit to The Hague to ask some pointed questions was in order.

His plan was to pose as a French official visiting the town. He had the clothes that he had used in Toulon, and he would take Matai with him as back up. He had an idea that the old lady who owned the farm where he got Blaez would help.

They landed on the same stretch of beach they did the last time and headed toward Scheveningen. They reached the farmhouse just after dawn. Blaez tagged along as he jumped overboard and swam after the boat when they tried to leave him behind.

They were noisily greeted by Blaez's mother and what Marty guessed was one of his sisters as they approached the gate. Both females stood their ground and told both the men and Blaez that they weren't welcome. But the farmhouse door opened, and the old lady, came out.

She stood looking at them for a long moment and then at the dogs. A look of surprise came over her face as she recognised him. She came down the path shooing the dogs out of the way and grabbed Marty by the shoulders, kissed him three times alternately on each cheek and said,

"Goode Morgen, hoe gaat het?"

"Madam," said Marty with a smile, "I am good."

She pointed to herself and said, "Vrouw Jongeline."

"Mrs. Jongeline, I am looking for Jeroen."

She shook her head to indicate she didn't understand.

"I am seeking, Jeroen," Marty tried again.

"Oh! u zoekt Jeroen!" she said with a sad look that said something was wrong.

"Where is he?" Marty asked.

"Hij werd gearresteerd en zijn met de Frans Consulaat," she said, pointing towards Den Haig.

Marty looked at Antton, who shrugged and then he realized what she meant. Jeroen had been arrested by the French secret police!

"Where?" he asked.

"Op het Frans Consulaat," she answered and that was close enough to French for him to realise she meant the French Embassy.

Madam Jongeline then mimed him being hit and fingernails being pulled out. "Damn he's been tortured," Marty realised.

"Thank you," Marty said then remembered a word Jeroen had used, "Bedanked!"

She laughed sadly, gave him a hug, and taking him by the arm, insisted,

"Com. Com," and led them into the house. She fed them breakfast of bread and cheese washed down with strong black coffee and gave Blaez a bowl of meat scraps.

Once they had eaten, she pulled a piece of paper out of a drawer and with a lump of charcoal, drew a map. She marked streets by name and a building she labelled as "politiebureau," which she then crossed out and looking them in the eyes, shook her head and waggled her finger. She then marked a second building marked "Frans Consulaat," she made a face and tapped it with her finger.

"Als hij nog in leven is, dat is waar je hem vindt."

Marty was tuning in and beginning to follow the gist of what she was saying. "If Jeroen is alive, that's where we will find him," he thought.

He thanked her, took the map, and folded it into his inside pocket. Finally, he stood, hugged her, and delivered three kisses.

She held him at arm's length by the shoulders and said,

"Veel geluk jounger."


They left and followed the road into The Hague, aiming to arrive in the general area of the map. In fact, it only took a couple of questions to locals to get into the right area. Marty noted that when he asked questions in French, most people looked him up and down as if he was something they had trodden in. *The French may have shown them 'liberty,' but it don't signify that they like them*, he thought.

They finally arrived outside a building festooned with French flags, and Marty told Matai to wait for him outside with Blaez.

Putting himself in the mindset that he had used in Toulon, he walked up to the front door and walked in. The guard looked at him in surprise, and Marty gave him 'a stop me if you want trouble' look that was simultaneously disdainful and superior.

He approached the desk and announced,

"I am Pierre Lamont of the Bureaux for Foreign Affairs, and I am here to interview the Dutch agitator Jeroen van Helden".

The person on the desk looked both surprised and afraid and asked him to wait while he consulted with the head of security. A couple of minutes later, he was back with a small man dressed in a black suit that was an almost identical match for Marty's.

"Monsieur Lamont, I am Federick La Plant, Head of Security for the Consulate. How can I help you?"

"As I told your – assistant – I am here to interview the Dutch agent."

La Plant looked at him for a long moment then said,

"Please come with me."

Marty was immediately on his guard as that was far too easy, but he followed along not having a better plan. La Plant led him deeper into the building and down some steps to the cellar. *Why do they always hold people in cellars?* Marty thought, *It must be something to do with dungeons.*

They came to a reinforced door that La Plant unlocked and stepped through. Inside the room was lit by several lamps.

There was a bed along one wall and chained to it was Jeroen. Marty almost didn't recognise him. His face was swollen and bruised, his naked torso was covered in cuts and burns, and his hands and feet were wrecked. They had pulled out his nails and systematically broken every bone. Then Marty noticed that he didn't blink. *Damn!* he thought, *they have cut off his eyelids!*

Marty fought to keep his composure and just stood looking dispassionate, but then he heard LaPlant slowly clapping his hands.

"Well done, Lieutenant. Your control is admirable," he said in English. "I see our little reception didn't stop you."

Marty looked around, saw he had a pistol pointed at him and said,

"So, you tortured him until he gave up everything he knew. But why did you go to all the trouble to try and trap me?"

"So, I could present you to the committee. They would value the gift of the one who stole their gold in Calais and smuggled the Dutch crown jewels out of the country. I will get a massive promotion and be a hero of the revolution," he stated in the same flat tone.

"How did you know they would send me and not just a Navy Frigate?"

"They would not want to expose their connection and you are their best undercover operative. You would be the logical choice."

"I'm flattered you think so highly of me," Marty replied.

Marty looked at Jeroen, who stared back at him with tears running down his face.

"Did you tell him about Jim?" he asked him. Jeroen shook his head.

Marty turned back to LaPlant, who said,

"Please drop your weapons on the floor," and pointed his gun at Marty's face.

Marty took the two stilettos from his sleeves and dropped them on the floor then took the pistols from his pockets and dropped them as well.

"Now, who is Jim?" LaPlant asked.

Jeroen sat upright and rattled his chain as he said,

"Why, that is his best friend, you asshole."

LePlant's eyes flicked towards Jeroen for just a split second but that was enough. Marty's hand flew back and then forward. Light glinted once on the blade of the fighting knife as it flew briefly through the air just before sinking to the hilt in LaPlant's throat. His eyes rolled up and he collapsed to the floor. The blade had severed the spine at the back of his neck.

Marty stepped forward and picked up his discarded weapons, put them back where they belonged, and pulled his knife out of the rapidly cooling corpse. He cleaned it on the dead man's coat and put it back in its sheath in the small of his back. He went to Jeroen and sat on the bed next to him.

"Who betrayed you?"

"A woman. Anouk van den Landen. She infiltrated the group and gave me to the French," Jeroen lisped through his broken teeth and lips.

"Where can I find her?"

"She lives in Rotterdam on Bredastraat. Will you avenge me?"

"Yes, you have my word."

They sat for a minute or two while Jeroen told Marty the story of the betrayal and gave a detailed description of his betrayer. He stopped often, obviously in great pain.

"Do you want to get out of here?" Marty finally asked.

"To do what?" Jeroen lisped through his swollen lips and broken teeth. "Live life a cripple? They broke my hands and feet amongst other things. No. I would like to die."

Marty smiled, reached out, and put his arm around his shoulders, pulling him to him. Jeroen looked at him and smiled, they stayed like that until he sighed and sagged down on the bed, dead.

Marty arranged the body and covered it with a blanket. You could hardly see the wound between the fourth and fifth rib where the stiletto had given Jeroen peace.

Marty had tears in his eyes as he picked up the pistol that LaPlant had dropped and checked the priming. He then took down the lanthorns. He blew one out and poured the oil around the room and over Jeroen's body, backing out of the door to leave a trail. He used the other to search the rest of the cellar. He found that while a couple of the other rooms were cells, one was full of papers, a cupboard full of brandy and the embassy's store of lamp oil. Perfect!

He poured several bottles of brandy around the room, took the lamp oil, and emptied all of it into the corridor. He backed up the stairs, turned the wick of the lamp up so the flame was good and long, and tossed the lamp on the floor.

The effect was satisfying. The oil ignited with a wumph, flames travelled down the corridor as he ran up the last few steps and burst out of the door. He made sure he left it open to allow a good draft to blow down the stairs.

As he ran, he yelled, "*FIRE,*" and bolted to the main door. He made it about halfway through the door when the world exploded.

# Chapter 5: Vengeance is mine

Matai was laughing at him as they walked back along the beach towards Nordwijk. Marty had lost his ponytail and most of the hair on the back of his head as he had been blown out through the front door of the Embassy.

What he hadn't known was that the French had stored a barrel of gunpowder in the cellar. When it exploded, the blast channelled up through the open door and into the foyer, blowing Marty out into the street with a fireball right on his heels. His clothes were on fire when he landed, and he had to roll around in the dirt to put them out. He ended up with burns on his head and neck, but it was nothing too serious and looked worse than it was.

Blaize walked ahead. He was obviously worried about his master, but the smell was bad enough to make him want to stay far enough away not to have to breath it. Marty didn't blame him, he smelt like a half-burnt corpse.

No one had tried to stop them leaving the town and the locals didn't seem to be making much effort to put out the embassy either. Rather, they focused on stopping the fire from spreading. It was a fitting pyre for his friend.

They reached the rendezvous and there was the Snipe hove to about a mile offshore. Matai waved as the boat was rowed in to pick them up. Once back on board, he went to his cabin and undressed. He had a standing bath with a bowl of warm water that Tom brought him and put on some clean trousers. He threw the burnt clothes out of the stern window to get rid of the stink.

Tom waited patiently while he did this then made him sit while he examined his burns.

"You will live. Though it will be a while before you can tie your hair back again. Do you want me to tidy it up?" he asked.

"Yes, please," Marty replied, "I need to be able to look at least respectable for when we go to Rotterdam."

"Rotterdam? I thought we would be going home."

"Unfinished business," Marty stated, "We need to pay a visit to Jeroen's betrayer. Once that's done, we can go back."

"It will be risky," Tom assessed, "How do you plan to do it?"

"It's a port. We will just sail in. We look like a neutral, so we will go in as one. Get a Swedish flag made up then set course for the harbour."

Tom set to work with a pair of shears and trimmed Marty's hair into a respectable shape. Once he was happy with it, he let Marty put on a shirt and jacket. Marty then rummaged around in his chest and pulled out a fisherman's cap, which he pulled on. It was sore wearing it, but it hid the bald patch.

"Will I pass?"

"You'll do."

One of the men, who was handy with a needle, made up a Swedish flag and once it was in place, they headed south. It only took a couple of hours to reach the docks and get moored on a buoy in the harbour. Marty, Tom, and Matai went ashore by boat and asked directions to Bredastraat.

Once there, they spread out to observe the address that Jeroen had given them. It wasn't long before a woman matching her description arrived in an open Landau and entered the house.

They waited. It started to get dark, lamps were lit along the street, and the house windows glowed with lantern or candlelight. They were about to move in when another carriage arrived. It was painted dark blue and was enclosed. The occupant got out and walked up the path. As he entered, the light cast by the lantern over the door, Marty could see he was dressed in the French style.

He knocked, and the door opened almost immediately, as if the person inside had been waiting for him. The woman they saw earlier was framed in the door and she greeted her visitor, as a lover, with a passionate kiss before he had even crossed the threshold.

Marty signalled for the boys to move in. Matai dealt with the driver of the carriage and Marty and Tom silently descended on the couple. Marty didn't hesitate but hit the embracing couple in a body tackle that threw the three of them onto the floor of the hallway in heap. Tom following behind, kicking the door shut.

Matai bundled the unconscious driver into the carriage, tied and gagged him, put on his coat and hat, and took his place on the driver's seat.

The woman shrieked, and the man was cursing in French. Tom stepped in and clipped him with his blackjack, knocking him unconscious. Marty quickly clamped his hand down over the woman's mouth, waved his knife in front of her eyes, and said "Shhhssshhh!"

Her unconscious lover was still laying on top of her, and Marty was on top of him. Marty had to slide to the side while keeping his hand over her mouth until Tom hauled the unconscious man out of the way. Marty had his blade on her neck the whole time.

It wasn't the most elegant of take downs, and it took a few moments to get themselves and their captives sorted out. Tom hog-tied the lover and gagged him. Marty took the woman into the drawing room, tied her hands and ankles, and gagged her. He then pulled the blinds so no one could look into the room from outside.

He took a breath and looked around the room. There was a desk with a leather chair, a couple of comfortable armchairs and a chaise long. He went to the desk and riffled through the papers on the top. There was a list of names on one sheet with Jeroen's at the top and Mrs. Jongeline halfway down. Several of the names had ticks against them.

He unlocked and searched the desk drawers. In one, he found a file. In it, written in French, was a copy of a report of how she had seduced Jeroen and used that to infiltrate the resistance group. There was a letter from La Plant telling her that her money would be paid in gold and that she was not to pass any information to anyone apart from him and 'Arnaud'.

He went over to Anouk and putting his mouth close to her ear, said softly in French,

"Is that Arnaud?"

She nodded.

"You know what happened to the embassy in The Hague?"

She shook her head.

"They had a fire and an explosion just after La Plant had a close encounter with this," he showed her the knife. "He died far too cleanly for my liking."

"They tortured my friend Jeroen so badly he begged me to kill him. I am very angry about that, and I swore to avenge him. You know that makes the chances of you surviving the night really small. Don't you?"

Her eyes got even wider.

"But how you die is up to you. You can come with us and tell me everything about what you know about the French intelligence network, and we will turn you over to British Intelligence. Or we can take you to our ship and I can have the crew take turns amusing themselves with you on our journey back to England until you will be begging me to let you jump overboard to drown yourself. In the end, you will still tell me everything."

He reached for the gag.

"But first, you will tell me who Arnaud is," he paused, "and don't try and lie or I will cut pieces off of him until you tell me the truth."

He pulled the gag away.

"He is my lover," she whispered.

"And what else?" Marty asked.

She didn't say anything, so Marty signaled to Tom and made a sign that could only mean 'cut off a finger'.

Tom went to the bound man and retied him, so he was spread-eagled with his arms along a pipe that ran along the wall. He kicked him a couple of times to wake him up and pulled out a tomahawk.

*Where did he have that hidden?* Thought Marty.

Tom then made a show of looking at Arnaud's hands, selecting the one with most callouses.

"Right-handed," he said happily and splayed the fingers out along the pipe.

"He is a member of French intelligence, and he is the brother-in-law of one of the committee members," she gasped.

Marty put the gag back on and said to Tom,

"We will take him with us as well."

They retied him so his hands were behind his back and Tom had him stand. Then, with his knife point pressed into his back, Tom pushed him out of the house and into the carriage.

Marty collected all the papers from the desk, untied Anouk's ankles, and pulled her to her feet. He suddenly had an urge to commit arson, picked up a lamp and threw it into the corner of the room by a set of heavy drapes. The oil spilled and caught fire immediately and when the flames took a hold of the drapes, he grabbed her by the arm and half-led, half-dragged her to the carriage.

As soon as they were aboard, Matai clucked the horses into motion and drove them back to the harbour. A look back showed flames licking the inside of the glass of Anouk's house, and Marty pulled her around by the hair so she could see it.

They got back to the Lark with all three prisoners without incident and as soon as the tide turned headed down the river Maas to get out to sea. The prisoners secured in the cable tier. They let the horse and carriage loose to make their own way home

Once they were out in the channel, Marty ordered Arnaud to be brought to his cabin.

He had arranged things very carefully. There was a chair for the prisoner to be tied in. Next to it, on the right, was a chopping block and a selection of hammers, knives, and tomahawks. The floor was covered in sand to catch any blood that was spilt and there was a small brazier of hot coals suspended by chains from a hook on the ceiling.

Marty had his desk set in front of the chair where he sat with paper and pen at the ready. The final touch were the two men who stood behind the chair. One was Burt Longbridge, a Marine that before he joined up had been a slaughter man and had one of the evillest faces Marty had ever seen. The other was Trevor Standish, who was renowned for his totally calm demeanor whatever came to pass and had the coldest washed out blue eyes that could pierce right through your soul.

Arnaud was brought in and lashed to the chair at his chest and shins, leaving his arms free.

Marty made a show of reading some papers, which had come from the house giving Arnaud plenty of time to look around and realise what the set up meant. He was banking on him believing they were prepared to do what his people had done to Jeroen.

"I want you to tell me your name and what is your position in the French secret service," Marty asked, putting down the papers.

Arnaud just looked at him.

"You know what they did to my friend, Jeroen?"

Still no reaction.

"Were you part of that?"

No answer.

He looked at his men and nodded. Trevor moved in and grabbed Arnaud's right hand and forced it down on the chopping block. Arnaud kept it fisted so Trevor pulled the fingers out by main strength and flattened them out. Burt then took a large nail and placed the point against the back of the hand and picked up a hammer.

*"Your name?"* Marty asked again.

Arnaud was sweating and pale but still said nothing.

Marty nodded, and the hammer came down, driving the nail through the hand into the block.

Arnaud screamed and started talking. He didn't stop talking for over two hours, by which time, Marty knew all about the French intelligence network in the Batavian Republic, its operatives, collaborators, and how they used what they knew to line their own pockets. Whenever he slowed, he had Trevor straighten out his fingers and Burt pick up a tomahawk. The pain from the nail grating against his bones and tendons was enough to get him talking again.

When he started repeating himself, Marty called a halt and had Burt pull the nail out, eliciting another scream. They locked him in the bread room after bandaging his hand.

Marty had the driver brought in and sat him in the chair. The man looked at the block, noted the fresh blood, and looked up at Marty with terror in his eyes.

"You speak French?" Marty asked.

"Yes," the man said.

"What is your name?"

"Peter. Peter van Sommoren."

"What was your job with the Frenchman?"

"I was Mr. Dubois' driver."

"For how long?"

"Just the last year."

This continued for several minutes until a name that hadn't been mentioned before came up.

"Who was that?" Marty asked.

"Mr. Mercier?"

"Yes."

"He came in from Paris. A member of the committee, I think. He was talking about how the factions were in danger of tearing France apart and that something needed to be done. They forget that the driver can hear everything that is said in the carriage."

"Did he say what needed to happen?"

"He said that it would be better if the group, that had taken over in June, removed the Jacobean faction. Leaving Sieyès, who is in charge of the directory, in total command. They have brought back Napoleon from Egypt to assist them."

"Have they bedamned!" said Marty out loud.

"When will all this happen?"

"He said they were aiming for November."

Marty kept calm with an effort. He thanked Peter van Sommoren and said he was free to take a walk around the deck.

Tom sat in a corner listening and said,

"That's very interesting. Do you think they know about this in London?

"I don't know," replied Marty, "but I think we need to tell them asap. Let's see what our femme fatale has to tell us.

Anouk was brought in and pushed down into the chair. She saw the block and the blood and her face paled.

"Where is Arnaud?" she asked in English.

*Interesting*, thought Marty, *she didn't do that before,* but he answered,

"He is down in the bilges. He may live to see tomorrow if you cooperate. He resisted but now he knows what poor Jeroen went through."

She paled even more, and her hands went to her mouth.

"He told me some interesting things." Marty continued checking his notes. "Now let's see if you can confirm some of them."

He asked her about the French Intelligence network in Holland, and she confirmed many of the things Arnaud had told him. Then he asked,

"Have you heard of or spoken to a Mr. Mercier?"

She said that she had met him through Arnaud, and he was someone important in Paris.

Marty then quizzed her about any conversations she had overheard and what was said. From what she told him, he basically confirmed everything the driver had told him but didn't get much more.

He had her taken back to the cable tier and sent for Arnaud again. He also got Burt and Trevor in again and had Tom sit in the corner to listen.

This time, he immediately asked about Mercier and the coup. Arnaud would say nothing. He had recovered his courage. Marty had him tied to the chair again and had Burt break two of his fingers.

The tap opened, and information poured out of him. It confirmed everything the others had said plus gave them some new names. When they had spent about three hours cross-checking and cross-examining, they let him go and put him back in the bread locker.

Marty was writing the last of his report when there was a knock on the door. A sailor entered and told him,

"John Smith says we is 'bout five miles off the estuary, sir." They were nearly home.

# Chapter 6: Insertion

Marty and Armand sat in Admiral Hood's office waiting for the Lord to finish reading Marty's report. As he finished each page, he passed it to William Wickham, the Spy Master, who was also reading every page with ferocious intensity.

Wickham suddenly looked at Marty and asked,

"All the hair on the back of your head?"

He twirled a finger for Marty to show him.

"Good gad!" he said when he saw the red healing skin.

He went back to reading.

Hood looked up and asked,

"Nailed his hand to a butchers block?"

Marty nodded, the good Lord shuddered, so Marty explained,

"I was angry."

Hood raised an eyebrow at that.

Twenty minutes and numerous comments later, Wickham put down the last sheet.

"Well, my boy, it seems that your act of vengeance has produced unexpected benefits. The news about the coup is very interesting," Wickham concluded.

Hood sat back in his chair staring at the ceiling and Marty thought, *he is looking old.* Hood's attention snapped back to the meeting as he looked at Wickham and said,

"Only one thing for it. We need someone on the ground in Paris to monitor this coup and to stir up the factions to keep the French off balance."

"Yes," replied Wickham, "If they get a stable government in place, they will be an even bigger threat than ever."

They turned as a pair and looked at Marty.

"Oh shit, what's coming now?" Marty thought but kept his features as calm as he could.

"You have a talent for working in enemy territory and now your hair is short, you could hardly be recognised as the boy in Toulon," said Wickham.

Marty said nothing. He just waited.

Wickham looked at Hood and stated,

"Linette is back from her latest sojourn. They work well together."

"Hmm, yes but methinks that this needs to be a three hander," said Hood. "Someone who can also bring a bit of muscle would be useful."

Marty looked at Armand, who shook his head.

"I am too well known in Paris mon cher," he explained, "How about Campbell?"

"Aah now. Mr. Campbell." Admiral Hood said thoughtfully.

"Campbell?" Wickham asked.

"Speaks French like a native. He is half French, y'know. Bare-knuckle fighter." He turned to Marty, "How's he been as part of your team?"

"Fits in, m'Lord," replied Marty, "Fights a ship and manages his men well. Brought the two prizes back under his command with a senior Mate running the second."

"His French is excellent, as you would expect, with a slight Burgundian accent. He would pass as a servant to Martin and Linette if we give them the cover of a married couple."

Marty coughed as his breath caught in his throat at that. *What would Caroline think of that,* he thought in a mild panic.

Wickham chortled at his reaction,

"Don't worry, my boy," he chuckled, "That vixen of a girlfriend of yours won't hear about it."

Caroline or 'Lady Candor' was Marty's love. She was a widow at twenty years old and extremely rich. Not that it mattered as he was independently wealthy himself, thanks to his prize money. She was tall, slender, shapely, auburn haired, and had green eyes that could turn cold grey when she was angry. He had fought a dual on her behalf where he killed her former lover. He was head over heels in love with her.

"Does she know about your work as an intelligence officer?" Asked Hood.

"She guessed I'm not an ordinary sailor and has visited The Farm, but we have never spoken of it and she doesn't ask questions," Marty answered.

"Not of you maybe, but she has given me more than one grilling," Hood harrumphed, "She damn well told me to my face that if I get you killed, she would personally see that my 'balls would be found in separate counties'."

Marty was quite red in embarrassment by now and proud at the same time.

"Quite a girl," laughed Wickham at Hoods discomfort, "maybe we could use her too?" he pondered.

"Now here!" Marty spluttered.

Wickham grinned and said, "Only joking my boy, only joking." With a short bark of a laugh. "But she would make a formidable weapon in the right hands."

"Now then," said Hood, pulling the subject back to business. "I think we are agreed. A team of three. Martin, Linette, and young Mr. Campbell. You have a little over a week to work up a cover story and get everything in place. We want you in Paris by the first of November, so you must leave the farm by the twenty-fifth. Linette will join you at the farm in three days. You can relax until then.

Relax? How the hell am I going to relax? Marty wondered.

He left the Admiralty and went to Caroline's house, but she wasn't at home. The servant said she was at her estates in Cheshire preparing the Christmas celebration she would throw for her tenants. Marty was frustrated in more ways than one and took a brisk walk to the de Marchet's house, via a chop house for lunch.

The Count was at home alone, as all the womenfolk and his son were on a shopping trip, so the two of them settled down next to the fire in the library with a bottle of Brandy between them.

"'ow did you burn your hair off like that?" The count asked when he saw the state of Marty's head.

"A small case off overlooking a powder keg when I was burning down the French Embassy in den Hague," he replied.

The Count nodded unperturbed by the revelation.

"I will probably get more details when I see Hood and William next time."

*William! First name terms with that rogue are you,* Marty thought.

"While I am here," Marty said softly, "can you tell me about Paris - where the government is based and the main ceremonial routes?"

"Now, why would you need to know that?" The Count asked with an amused look.

"I am sure 'William' will tell you when you see him next," Marty retorted.

The Count laughed.

"My, you have grown up fast. What happened to that cabin boy I sponsored?"

"He had to grow up fast before 'William' managed to kill him," Marty reposted with a grin.

"Touché!" laughed the Count and started giving Marty a detailed briefing on the revolutionary government, where it was run, and the route they took to parade their heroes. He had a map, which he pointed everything out on.

Two and a half hours later, they heard the front door open and an excited Antoine, the count's young son, rushed in followed by the countess and her daughter Evelyn. He could see a couple of servants in the hall outside struggling with a pile of packages.

He knelt and hugged the young boy, who looked at his head with wide eyes.

"Where is your 'air?" he asked.

"Oh, that's a mighty tale," teased Marty, "It was sacrificed for King and Country!"

"Can you tell it to me as a bedtime story?" Antoine pleaded.

"As long as he keeps it short," said the countess indulgently, looking fondly at the two of them.

"Madam," Marty said as he stood to embrace her, kissing her on either cheek.

"Evelyn." He hugged her and kissed her cheeks as well.

"'ow is Caroline?" she asked archly, knowing full well if she was in town, Marty would be in her bed.

"In the country setting up a do for her tenants," he replied, "I would go there, but I have to be back at our base in two days."

"Another mission?" asked the countess with concern. "You 'ave just returned from the last one, and you are 'urt!"

"Not seriously" Marty re-assured her. "The hair will grow back quickly. And I have a few days before we leave again."

"I suppose where you are going is a secret? Don't answer! Your face says it all," Evelyn snipped, a little put out not to be the centre of attention.

"Of course, it is. That's the way it works," Marty grinned at her.

"Now, don't ask questions of poor Martin you know he can't answer," chided the Count.

"Well, will you be back for Christmas or my wedding?" Evelyn asked. Marty didn't miss the pleading, concerned look in her eyes.

"I think I will be back by then," he said, "but you know the Navy. Nothing is ever certain."

They dropped the subject then as a servant announced that dinner was about to be served.

Marty stayed the night. He didn't forget his promise to Antoine and told him a story of spies and daring do. In the morning, he made his excuses and returned to the farm.

Back at the farm, he got an enthusiastic and wet greeting from Blaez, who insisted on pinning him down in a chair and washing his head. Then he curled up on his lap and went to sleep. Now having half a hundredweight of dog go to sleep on your lap can keep you warm, but it can also give you dead legs. Then, when he starts dreaming of chasing rabbits and his legs twitch like he is running, it can get somewhat uncomfortable as dog claws and human skin aren't a good match. So, it was with a small amount of relief when Tom walked in, and Blaez woke and jumped down to greet him.

Tom pulled up a chair and sat.

"I just talked with Armand."

Marty waited for what he knew was coming next.

"You be going into Paris with Miss Linette and Mr. Campbell. That be one of the stupidest things I heard for a while," he said with concern.

"Oh, I don't know," Marty said thoughtfully, "Me blowing myself up must compare."

Tom laughed and looked at Marty's hair.

"You do look a bit of a fool at that." He smiled. "But all the same. Paris? That be like walking into the lion's den."

"Look," Marty said, to reassure him it wasn't a fool's errand, "the French Government is about to try to go through a massive change. We need to disrupt that to make sure they stay fighting amongst themselves. If they get organized, we could be in real trouble."

"Can't imagine them Frenchies ever getting organized," Tom grumbled but he knew when he was flogging a dead horse, so he let it go.

The next morning, a very small man with ink-stained hands arrived and said he was from the 'Ministry'. He had a wooden chest with him which opened out into a writing desk. From a drawer, he produced several sheets of paper, and, from another, a pot of ink sealed with a cork. He asked for both Marty and James to be present.

"This paper is exactly the same as used by the authorities in France to issue identity documents and permits," he explained, "The ink is also exactly the same as used by their clerks, as is the quill. I can reproduce the handwriting of the actual clerks in different departments, and I am familiar with the layout and wording of all their documents."

He selected a sheet of paper that was a bit more ragged than the rest and asked, "What is your intended entry point into France and your route to Paris?"

"I thought we might land at Hornfleur," Marty started but the little man tutted and shook his head.

"Might I suggest that with your wounds, you pose as a wounded naval officer returning after being exchanged. Arriving in Le Havre with your Coxswain. You will meet your wife there and leave for Paris by coach travelling via Rouen and Gisors. That would be the expected route and explain you suddenly popping up."

"Alright and who will I be?" asked Marty thinking, *Why do I get the feeling this has all been thought out for me?*

"We have captured a French lieutenant who matches you for looks close enough that you could pass for him. And the wounds will cover any differences. He is too badly wounded to be exchanged and will probably die in England. So, we will exchange you instead," the little man replied.

"And if we bump into any of his family?" Marty asked.

"No chance of that," he replied as he examined the nib of his pen. "They are from Montpellier, and the chances of them travelling to Paris are miniscule."

Marty thought about that for a while and said,

"That sounds like it could work, but I will need to learn his background, what ships he served on, how he was captured."

The little man raised a finger and delved into the drawers again. After a moment of rummaging, he came up with a packet, which he handed to Marty.

"All you need is in there. Almost forget to give it to you," He laughed, sounding more like a braying donkey than a man.

"And how will my 'wife' get over to France?" Marty enquired.

"Oh, she is already there. Left yesterday and will arrive in Le Havre in three days' time."

Just then, Campbell walked in, having been summoned from the dock, and looked at the little man quizzically.

"Mr.?" Marty looked at the man enquiringly.

"Oh, didn't I introduce myself? Thelonious Friar at your service."

"Mr. Friar let me introduce Midshipman James Campbell. My 'cox' for this mission."

"Ah, the fighter," Friar quipped, "I will start with you. French identity documents contain a description of the subject."

Campbell looked at Marty with raised eyebrows and a 'what the hell is going on?' look on his face.

"We haven't briefed mister Campbell yet as he has just returned from a family visit," Marty explained to Friar, then to Campbell.

"We have a mission in Paris, and you are coming with me James." If anything, Campbell's eyebrows went up even higher.

"Oh, right, Paris? Wow!" He said in surprise.

Marty laughed and opened the packet.

Inside was a sketch of the French officer, whose name was Sebastian St Martin and had the rank of Enseigne de Vaisseau de Première Classe, formerly of the Frigate Immortalité that was captured by the British at Tory Island. They were right, he could be Marty's brother.

Marty looked through and found another set of papers for a Frederique Le Bonne, who was a Premiere Maitre (First Mate). He had died in custody and came from the same ship. He passed them to Campbell.

"Dead man's shoes," Campbell joked.

Friar looked at the two of them like he was their schoolmaster and cautioned,

"You both need to be totally familiar with your characters as you may well be questioned by the authorities."

They both returned a look that said, 'you don't say!' He started to write out an identity document, frequently looking up to examine Campbell or Marty and noting some feature or other.

Marty read through the file, passing relevant sheets to Campbell as he finished them.

"What of the other officers on the Immortalité?" asked Marty.

"Either killed or exchanged. We kept track of the ones we exchanged as we were curious if the French were honouring their Parole. They aren't, of course, and all the officers are back on serving ships."

"So, there isn't much chance that I will bump into any of them?"

"Not much, but I'm sure you will be able to deal with them if you do."

Campbell looked up from the sheets he was reading and asked,

"So, what are we to do once we are in Paris?"

"What we do best, cause trouble," Marty grinned. "We need to stir up trouble between the factions and stop one of them getting the upper hand."

Friar dusted the document he had just finished and set it to one side. He took up another piece of paper and looked critically at Marty.

"How did you set your head on fire?" He asked.

"You mean you don't know. Tssk," Marty replied then asked, "Who are our contacts in Paris?"

Friar gave him a steady look but let that one pass.

"Your 'wife' will introduce you to all of them. I understand you have worked together before?"

"Yes, in Amiens and Toulon."

"Mr. Wickham said you work well together."

*Was that the trace of a smirk?* Thought Marty.

Marty went to a cabinet on the far side of the room and opened the doors. Inside on several shelves were a variety of pistols and knives. He selected two pairs of pistols. One was of fine quality with silver chasings, the other plainer and more workman like. He then picked up and discarded several knives until he found the ones he wanted. He laid all these out on the table then went back and selected powder flasks and bullet moulds from another drawer.

He called Campbell over and pushed the two plainer pistols and a couple of knives towards him.

"Make yourself familiar with them and get John Smith to fit you with concealing sheaths for the blades." He returned to the cabinet a third time and returned with a pair of Garrottes and a shepherd's sling.

He turned around to say something to Friar when he saw the man was frozen in his seat with Blaez standing on his hind legs, his front paws on the writing chest glaring at him with his hackles up.

"Down Blaez," Marty commanded and whistled softly. Blaez looked over his shoulder at him, looked back at Friar, growled, and did as he was told.

"Damn and Blast!" Said Friar, "Where did that beast come from?"

Marty deliberately misunderstood the question and said, "Holland."

Friar's mouth opened and closed as he considered a retort but couldn't think of one.

"He will be coming with us," Marty stated and when Friar looked to object, he said with a completely straight face, "It's alright, he speaks perfect French."

There was a snort of supressed laughter from Campbell and a clack of teeth as he tossed Blaez a piece of ship's biscuit, which he crunched noisily.

Friar stayed with them for two days, during which he quizzed them on their characters until he was happy, they had them down pat. He prompted Marty to show him the weapons he had selected and was surprised when he saw that they had all been made in France. He asked to see the fighting knife, and Marty obliged him, pointing out that it was made in America and that a Frenchman could obtain one from any of the American ships that broke the blockade.

The time came to leave, and they were taken by carriage to Chatham, where a Merchantman was being loaded with French army and navy officers who were being exchanged. There weren't many, and they were able to stay slightly apart. Marty had his head bandaged, and Campbell hovered around him as if he was caring for him. Blaez laid down at his feet and growled at anyone who got too close or looked as if they would approach. His presence was enough to keep any casual approaches at bay.

The trip across to Le Havre didn't take long. The weather was reasonable, and the wind cooperated. When they arrived, they moored rather than docked and the port authority ferried them ashore. Blaez thought that was great. He jumped from the deck down into the boat startling the oarsmen and then stood at the bow with his front paws on the gunnel as if he owned the boat.

When they came up on the dock, Blaez jumped ashore before they had tied off and was yipping and wuffling as he greeted Linette. Running around her and jumping up for a neck scratch. Marty was 'helped' up the steps by Campbell, and they made a show of the brave sailor being greeted by his caring wife.

Linette had organised a carriage to take them to Paris and as soon as they were in and on their way, Marty asked very quietly,

"Can we trust the driver?"

"No, he is not one of our people, he came with the coach," she replied.

Marty nodded and looking at Campbell, pointed up and then placed a finger on his lips. James nodded.

To fill the time, they chatted about the latest news in Paris, Linette filling them in on the political situation, obliquely wrapping it up in general conversation. In the end, they fell to snoozing. Blaez curled up on Marty's left with his head on his lap, and Linette on his right with her head on his shoulder.

# Chapter 7: Paris

They arrived in Paris on the first of November as planned. It was late afternoon as they pulled up outside of the house Linette had rented. James tipped the driver and carried their meagre possessions inside.

As always, when in enemy territory, they always spoke French.

"The house is just off the Rue Honoré," Linette said. "It is very near the route that a hero like Napoleon would take to make a grand entrance onto the city." She led them into the main room downstairs. "This is what you would call the drawing room. There is a dining room next door and a kitchen at the back. There are three bedrooms upstairs."

"One each then," grinned Marty.

"Yes," replied Linette with a smirk. "I have no intention of incurring the wrath of your girlfriend."

"Ouch," chipped in James, "That was to the point."

"Naturally," Linette responded, "We have to work together now and maybe in the future. His lover is quite capable of hiring an assassin if she thinks her man is being taken from her arms."

"Oh, she's not that bad," Marty quipped, "She would probably just hire someone to rough you up."

James rolled his eyes and wondered what the hell he had gotten into.

They settled in quickly, and Marty carried out a perimeter check for access points that needed to be secured, and for escape routes. He rigged alarms with bottles and cords on the rear door and the cellar hatch that would alert them to forced entries. He also took measures to prevent someone opening the ground floor windows with a slim jim. The cellar had an old tallboy cabinet that he turned into an armoury as he planned on increasing their stock of weapons locally.

Their first task was to contact the local agent who would brief them on the current political situation. First thing in the morning of the second of November, they went to Notre-Dame Cathedral where they had a rendezvous setup. The agent would be standing by the Point Zero des Routes de France at nine.

.

They decided that Marty and James would arrive early and set up as an observation team to make sure that the agent wasn't being followed or that there weren't any unwanted observers around. When they gave the allclear, Linette would make contact and take the agent to a café where they could sit and talk. The boys would shadow them and run interference if there was a problem to allow them to split up and get away.

At eight thirty, Marty wandered into the Parvis with Blaez at his side and positioned himself so he could see both the Parvis and the Rue del la Cité. James sat in a café on the corner of the Rue d'Arcole where he could observe the other approaches.

Linette waited in another café for the all-clear. She wore a simple dress, that was fashionable but not expensive, and a cloak with a hood that hid her face. It was cold and snowing gently so no one would think it odd that she kept the hood up during the initial contact.

Both Marty and James spotted the contact walking into the square towards the point zero triangular stone marker. He was carrying a blue book under his left arm as identification. They carefully scanned both in front and behind him as well as to all sides, looking for anyone suspicious that could be observing the square or following the agent. They also checked any windows that overlooked the Parvis and the roof lines.

Having completed his scan, Marty looked over to James, who picked up a newspaper and started to read, the sign for the all-clear. Marty took off his hat and wiped the rim, signalling Linette that it was alright to move.

She left the café and walked over to point zero greeting the agent like he was a relative with a kiss on either cheek. What no one else could hear was the exchange of recognition phrase and response that was whispered between kisses. She kept her hood up as an extra precaution.

They walked arm in arm back to the café and sat inside by the window. Marty and James moved to positions outside where they could keep watch. They had selected the café carefully as it couldn't be approached covertly. and it had a back door that could be used as an escape route if needed.

The meeting lasted around half an hour then they stood, embraced again, and left in opposite directions. Back at the house, Marty and James arrived back after Linette. They had monitored her back trail for anyone following. They were frozen and headed to the fire to warm up.

Linette sat in a comfortable chair reading the blue book.

"Anything interesting?" Marty asked.

"Yes. There are two main factions: The Jacobins and The Royalists. The Directorate of five holds power after a Coup in June when they overthrew the Jacobins. The Directorate is run by Emmanuel Joseph Sieyès an ex-priest who wrote the 3rd Estate. They are afraid the Jacobins will make a comeback. There are rumours that they want to get Napoleon on the Directorate to strengthen their position. Bonaparte's brother Lucien is the President of the Council of Five Hundred and will play a big role in that."

"So, what can we do to stir things up and destabilize them then?" Asked Marty.

"The obvious thing is to create more tension between the factions," Linette suggested, "If we do that, they may tip over into open conflict and rip each other apart."

"So, we need to plant evidence that hints that the Jacobins are about to do something like a counter coup then," suggested James.

"Something like that might do it," Marty agreed.

The next day, Marty, or rather Sebastian St. Martin, had a visit from a Ministry of Marine courier ordering him to present himself at the Ministry the next day for a debriefing. He immediately began to review their back story in his mind and make sure he had the answers to all the questions he could think of. He would have to improvise any others.

Linette went out and met the local contact to discuss their idea for fermenting distrust between the factions. James went with her to make sure the meeting wasn't observed.

When they returned flushed from the cold, she had news. Rumours were already spreading that the Jacobins were preparing a coup. The contact was of the opinion it would take very little to push the Directorate into taking punitive measures. That, they calculated, would force the Jacobin faction into retaliation and they could see the whole thing escalate into open conflict. Perfect.

Marty reported to the ministry as required in the morning. He wore a loose bandage around his head to protect it from the cold and because it emphasised his status as a wounded warrior. He wasn't surprised to find the reception he got was very similar to that at the Admiralty. The waiting room was manned by a clerk, who had an elevated opinion of himself and his status and treated the sailors with disdain.

He looked down his nose at Marty, who introduced himself and passed him his orders. The clerk wrote a note, which he gave to a messenger, who went off to deliver it to whoever he was supposed to meet.

He waited for well over an hour, during which he read the newspapers that were left on the central table. He was lucky that a 'fellow officer' took pity on his wounded colleague and gave up his chair for him.

Eventually, another messenger arrived, and he was led deep into the building. He was shown into a room and was confronted with what looked like the setting for his Lieutenant's exam. There were three men sitting behind a desk, two in civilian suits and the third in the uniform of a Navy Captain. The room was windowless, painted in a drab beige, and lit by several lanterns, which just made it stuffy. It didn't help that one of the civilians was puffing foul-smelling smoke out of a clay pipe.

He was pointed to a wooden chair, and he sat down facing the three.

"You are Sebastian St. Martin Enseigne de Vaisseau de première classe, of the Frigate Immortalité?" Asked the man in the middle.

"Yes, I am."

"You were captured by the British at Tory Island?"

"I was."

"Please tell us what happened and how you happened to be captured."

Marty knew the whole battle by heart and recited the narrative he had prepared, making it sound as if the recollection was painful to him. He finished by saying he was hit by an exploding powder carrier and was knocked out. He had regained consciousness in the surgeon's quarters of the Fisgard, who had captured them just outside of Brest.

"Your Captain was killed?"

"Yes, he died on the quarterdeck with the first."

"What was the condition of the ship when it surrendered?"

"I am told it was sinking."

"You were told?"

"When we arrived in England and I was released from hospital, I was put with some other officers and servants. One of those was a cox from the Immortalité. He told me."

"What was his name?"

"Frederique Le Bonne. He was exchanged with me and is here in Paris as my companion and helper."

The civilian on the end went through some papers then nodded to the man in the centre.

All this time, the officer listened with a bored look on his face as if he had heard it all before. He looked at Marty narrow-eyed and asked,

"Please remove your bandage and show us your head."

Marty was surprised but did as he was asked, commenting,

"It is only there to protect my head from the cold."

He stood and turned his back to the three.

"Were you hurt anywhere else?" the officer asked.

"Yes, I was burnt on my back."

He made as if he was about to remove his coat.

"It is sufficient that we see your head," the man in the middle said.

"You may sit down."

Marty sat and looked steadily at the three of them and made no attempt to replace the bandage.

"Are you still in pain?"

"Yes, I have headaches and my vision sometimes goes blurred. The doctors say it is the remains of the shock to my brain."

"So, you are not fit to return to sea?"

"They say I am not."

The second civilian checked another set of papers and nodded again to the man in the middle. The three then had a whispered discussion. The chairman (as Marty was thinking of him) sat forward with his arms on the table and said,

"You will report to the ministry tomorrow. We will place you in the Supply Department until you can return to sea duty. Le Bonne will be ordered to report for duty as soon as a suitable post is found."

He looked at Marty for several seconds.

"Your orders will be delivered this afternoon. You may go."

Marty stood and went to the door. The same messenger was waiting outside ready to guide him out.


Back at the house, he found Linette and James and gave them a brief report on what happened.

"What do we do if I get orders?" James asked.

"You will have a 'tragic accident' in between here and the ship, and a body will be found that looks enough like you beside the road to prevent further investigation," answered Linette, "You will be back in England at the farm by then."

Marty looked thoughtful.

"I might be able to intercept any orders or remove James from the list while I am in the ministry. I will need a few days to see how that goes. Meantime, what are we going to do to stir things up?"

"We need the directorate to get nervous," Linette suggested.

"An assassination attempt on one of them?" James put in.

"That might work but how?" Marty asked.

They argued back and forth different ideas from a raid on a member's house, discounted as too risky as the members were heavily guarded by police, to a long range shot with a musket.

They finally decided that a small bomb would be their best bet as it would send a message and didn't have to kill the target, just get close. Marty had reservations about the collateral risks, as he didn't like to kill civilians unnecessarily, but he rationalised that if they saved British lives as a result, then it would be worth it.

The next day, Marty reported to the ministry as ordered and ended up sitting at a plain wooden desk with one drawer that didn't lock. He sat in a very uncomfortable wooden chair. A snotty-nosed, spotty individual dropped a pile of reports and a ledger on his desk, and he was told to enter the details from the reports in the ledger against the ship's name.

Within thirty minutes, he was bored to tears. Paperwork was never his forte. He could fill in the Admiralty forms necessary to keep a ship running if he had to, but this was tedious beyond belief. He looked around the office where there were another five men doing the same thing. They were all veterans and all recovering from wounds of varying severity.

He looked across at a one-armed lieutenant who was obviously as disinterested in his task as he was. The lieutenant looked back at him and grinned.

"Exiled here with the rest of us cripples hey?" he asked.

"Yes, unfit to be sent back to a ship, so punished by a whip made of paper," Marty quipped.

"Raymond de Lyon late of the Herculese." The one-armed man introduced himself.

"Sebastian St. Martin of the Immortalité," Marty replied in kind.

Raymond looked him over.

"You seem to have your full complement of wings and pins so what stops you from sailing?"

"Oh, I got blown up," said Marty, turning his head to show his red scalp and slowly growing hair. "A full charge from a nine-kilogram cannon went up in its carrier box right behind me. Poor boy was blown to bits. I was blown across the deck and was only saved from going overboard by the boarding nets," he explained, "I spent a while in an English hospital before being exchanged back to France at the end of October. How about you?"

"Oh, I got hit by a musket bullet, and it smashed my arm. They took what was left off, and now I'm stuck here." Raymond looked around furtively and then took a flask out of his jacket pocket. "Fancy a drop of Brandy? Makes the day go much quicker."

"Don't mind if I do." Marty grinned.

Two hours later, Marty had done very little paperwork but had found out a lot about the layout of the ministry and how there was a regular tyrant in charge of the section that posted exchanged men to ships. He was purported to be an ex-school master from the Naval college in Brest and was rumoured to have an intense dislike of all junior officers.

At the end of the day, he loitered behind and waited for the others to leave. He made his way to the part of the building that Raymond had told him the postings office was in and looked for the right door. Luckily, like most government organisations the Ministry was obsessed with labelling everything, so he soon found what he was looking for.

He knocked on the door and when there was no answer, he took a quick look up and down the corridor and gently opened it. There was no one inside, so in he went. There were several cupboards and a desk. The desk had a couple of paper trays on it with neatly stacked papers in them.

He had just started leafing through the top one when the door opened behind him and a voice asked,

"And what the hell are you doing in here?"

He turned and saw a short, older man with grey hair and a pugnacious look on his face.

*"I was – aahh,"* he started to say.

"Looking to see if you were going to be posted to a ship." The man finished for him, "You young officers are all the same. Impatient, reckless, and foolhardy." He paused and looked Marty up and down. "You are recovering from being wounded and they put you here to do some paperwork while you recuperate?"

"Yes, sir," replied Marty

"What is your name? You look familiar."

"Sebastian St. Martin, sir," Marty replied.

"Ha! I thought so! You were at the college at Brest in '91. I taught you Algebra. Mr. Dagmey, do you remember me?"

Marty thought fast. He couldn't deny this as he knew that Sebastian had gone to Brest Naval College.

"Of course! I didn't recognize you, sir. It's been a long time, and I have trouble remembering things since I was hurt," he improvised.

"Well, I can save you the trouble of looking," Dagmay said as he walked behind the desk and took a sheet of paper from the lower tray.

"Let me see...... Yes, you are on the list of those that are wounded but will return to duty eventually. Hmm, you were exchanged recently?"

"Yes, sir. At the end of October."

"Then you would not be sent back to sea for a couple of months anyway as it takes time to send back the officer you were exchanged for." He sighed. "I have a backlog of papers to process. It will take me a month to catch up"

Marty thought fast.

"Maybe I could help you, sir. They just have me entering reports now and that isn't very... well," he stuttered to a stop.

"Interesting," Dagmay finished for him, "Maybe you could at that, you were one of my brighter students. Report here tomorrow morning. I will take care of the transfer."

# Chapter 8: The Best Intentions

Marty got back to the house an hour later and was going to tell them the good news when he caught the unmistakable odour of gunpowder. He went into the kitchen and found Linette and James with an open barrel of fine gunpowder, the type used for pistol or musket loads, on the table. He quickly looked around, checking for open flames, and finding none approached them.

"For the bomb?" he asked.

"Yes," replied James, "It's the best we could get. At least, it's better than the stuff they put in their ships."

Marty rubbed some between his fingers feeling the grade of the grains and then carefully brushed his fingers off into the barrel.

"It should do just fine," he said, "What are we putting it in to make a bomb?"

"There are four kilograms in this barrel. How much do you think we should use?" asked Linette.

"Four pounds, two kilograms, would be more than enough," said Marty, "so about half of this."

Linette went to a cupboard and brought back a cast iron casserole dish with a lid. "Would this do it?"

"I like your thinking," Marty replied and took the pot from her. "If we fill this and wrap it in rope to hold the lid on it will make a hell of a bang. The question is how do we set it off?"

"I've been thinking about that, and we can't use slow fuse as the smoke and smell will give it away. I was wondering if we could use a flintlock or wheellock somehow and trigger that with a long cord," James said.

"That means one of us would have to be nearby when we set it off. It would be better if we could fire it off automatically," Marty said thoughtfully.

They threw ideas back and forward over dinner and the discussion continued until they went to bed, but they didn't come up with anything.

On his way to the ministry the next morning, he was passing by a shop and was surprised when what he took to be model of an acrobat on a trapeze suddenly started to move. It was an automaton, and it performed a whole routine before going back to its rest position. That set him thinking.

He reported to the posting's office and Dagmay gave him a pile of reports on exchanged sailors to sort and classify. He then had to create a list with the names, ranks, last ship and state of readiness of those fit to be reposted. He was about halfway through sorting the reports when he came upon the file for *Frederique Le Bonne*. He put him in the pile of 'unfit to be posted' sailors until Dagmay left the room and then slipped it into a hidden pocket at the back of his coat. That taken care of, he continued with his allotted task until it was time to go home.

When he got to the house, it was empty except for Blaez who greeted him as normal. He took him out for a walk and looked in at a couple of clock shops on his way, an idea percolating in the back of his mind.

He got back to the house and found Linette and James in the kitchen preparing dinner. The casserole was on the table. Linette looked worried and before Marty could tell them he had secured James's papers, she said,

"Something is about to happen in the next couple of days. Napoleon's brother, who is the chairman of the Councils, is spreading rumours of a rebellion. Napoleon has started positioning troops quietly around the city. If we do something it must be tonight or tomorrow." She stopped what she was doing and said, "Napoleon will be at the ministry of war tomorrow morning."

"Are you suggesting we go after him?" Marty asked in surprise.

"No, but his brother will be leaving his house at the same time and would be an easier target with all eyes on the General."

"The bomb?" Marty asked.

James leaned forward from where he was sitting the other side of the table.

"This is no good," he said, pointing at the casserole. "It's too heavy and too hard to get into place. It would also cause a lot of innocent casualties as his house is near a school."

Marty nodded.

"We need something that can be in plain sight and won't attract attention, is easy to position and can be set off at a distance."

"A box of empty wine bottles," Linette suddenly offered.

The boys looked at her quizzically.

"Everybody puts out their empty wine bottles to be collected by the road so that the wine shops can re-use them. The bottles cost more than the wine most of the time."

"So, we disguise our bomb as a box of empty bottles and leave it outside his house. But how do we set it off at the right time?" Marty asked.

"If we placed a closed lantern in the top of the box and some loose powder below you could shoot the lantern and that would do it," James suggested.

"That would be quite a shot even if we can find a vantage point," Marty said.

"Then we should go and have a look this evening," Linette said.

After dinner, they took a walk across town to the home of Lucien Bonaparte. It was in a nice suburb in a row of typical town houses that faced onto the road and had courtyards at the back. Walking up the road, Marty looked for somewhere that someone with a musket could hide to detonate the bomb. There wasn't anywhere. That plan wouldn't work.

Back at the house, they revisited the problem and concluded that all they could do was set a slow fuse in the box and light it just before they placed it outside of his house. The hardest part would be distracting the police guards to enable the switch. They would just have to hope no one would smell it.

Six o'clock the next morning saw the three of them near the house. Linette and James were dressed in typical low-income clothes and had used make-up to change their appearance (France was supposed to be classless, but in reality, there were still strata in their society) and went first. They had both sloshed wine over their clothes to reinforce the impression that they were on their way home after a good night out. As they got near to the house, they started to argue loudly and drunkenly. They got increasingly rowdy the closer they got, reaching a peak just outside the door.

The police guards moved in to move them on and made a real attempt to quiet them as they didn't want the chairman's rest to be disturbed. As they allowed themselves to be moved away, they resisted just enough to keep the guards focus on them. That allowed Marty to walk up to the door and switch his box for the one that was already there. Then he just walked on.

A half hour later, Lucien's coach appeared ready to take him to the Council. One of his servants opened the front door when the bomb went off shattering windows up and down the street and demolishing the rear of the carriage. The terrified horses bolted off down the street and disappeared into the distance to be stopped eventually by a teamster who was walking to work. The two police guards were killed instantly as was the servant and the carriage driver. Several people were hit by flying glass.

All in all, as a terror attack it had the right impact but not the expected result. Lucien used it as ammunition the following day to persuade the councils that there was a Jacobin revolt going on in Paris and persuaded them to decamp to the Chateaux de Saint-Cloud. Bonaparte was given charge of all military assets in the area and charged with their safety.

Three of the five councils resigned in protest leaving only Napoleons allies remaining.

The next day, Napoleon walked into the Council backed by a contingent of grenadiers. He was attacked by a group of councillors despite that, prompting Lucien to order the military to disband the council on the excuse there was an open rebellion.

The trap had snapped shut.

Napoleon had pulled off a Coup d'état.

# Chapter 9: Rumbled

The team sat in their house wondering what the hell went wrong. Instead of stirring up conflict between the factions, it looked like they had triggered a military coup. They weren't to know it was a coincidence.

The ministries were closed, so Marty didn't have to go to work. The city was under martial law and a strict curfew was being enforced. All they could do was sit it out.

Six days later, Napoleon had consolidated his position and was officially made First Consul. The curfew was lifted. The team got their heads down and tried to get as many facts about the sequence of events together as they could.

Then a bombshell landed or rather knocked at the door. James answered it and walked back into the drawing room with a young woman in a travel-stained cloak.

"May I introduce Madam St. Martin, the wife of Sebastian," he announced.

You could cut the silence in the room with a knife.

She looked around the room and at Marty and Linette and said,

"Who are you? Where is my husband?"

Linette reacted first and asked her to step into the dining room where she would explain. She took the confused woman by the hand and led her through the door.

Marty looked at James and said,

"Well, that's torn it! We had better get ready to leave."

It didn't take them long as they kept escape kits ready. They had just come down from upstairs when Linette came out of the dining room with a tearful Madam Saint Martin in tow.

"I have explained the situation to Maria, and she will be accompanying us back to England."

"What?" Blurted Marty in English.

"My husband was still alive when you left?" Maria asked.

"Well, yes he was," Marty said, "He was wounded and in hospital, but he was alive."

"Then I want to go to him and be with him," Maria stated with determination, "I have travelled here from the other end of France to find him. I heard from the cousin of one of his teachers at the college in Brest that he was here."

Alarm bells went off in Marty's head. Dagmay!

"Where are you staying?" Marty asked.

"At the house of Monsieur Dagmay," she replied.

"He asked me to go to this house to meet you."

*And I told him my wife was here with me. Damn!* Marty thought.

"We have to leave now!" Marty said.

The three exchanged a look and started moving at the same time. Marty threw packs to the other two and Linette led the way through the kitchen and down into the cellar. Maria was behind her looking bewildered followed by James then Marty. Blaez, who had picked up on the change in mood, stuck to Marty's side and was on high alert.

As they went down the steps to the cellar, there was suddenly the sound of banging on the front door and shouting. Blaez tensed, but Marty quieted him with a touch and a whispered command, then closed and bolted the cellar door. He stretched a string across from the door handle to the trigger of a pistol set so that if anyone opened the door the pistol would fire into the barrel of gunpowder lodged just to the side of it. He pulled the hammer back to full cock and followed the others. When he got to the cabinet where he kept his weapons, he picked up a carpet bag filled it with weapons and slung it over his shoulder.

While this was going on, James moved a couple of old tables that were propped up against the wall and revealed a door through to the adjoining cellar. He had it open and was waiting for Marty to come through before shutting and barring it from the other side.

Linette had a lanthorn lit and led the way through the cellar to a set of steps that went up to a hatch. Marty put Blaez on his lead to stop him running ahead and James opened it. The hinges were well oiled and made no sound. He took a long look around and made a signal for them to wait. He silently moved up the steps and out of the hatch. Thirty seconds later, he returned and beckoned them forward.

They emerged into a courtyard, and Marty noticed a body in the corner with its head at a very strange angle. It looked like James hadn't taken any chances.

Marty took Maria by the arm as if they were out for a stroll and led her out of the gates and down the road towards the river. James followed a couple of minutes later. They were now two couples not a party of three.

Down at the river, Marty walked along the bank to the Quay de la Tuileries. He was just thinking that the police hadn't thought to check the cellar when there was the sound of an explosion from behind them.

He picked up the pace a little and took some steps down from the road to a floating dock on the river. There were several pleasure craft moored up and he went to one with a mast and a covered cabin.

Once inside, he quickly changed into clothes the rivermen typically wore and pulled on a loose-fitting woollen cap. James and Linette came down and joined them just as Marty went back up on deck and started preparing the boat to leave. Blaez was firmly told to stay below when he tried to follow Marty on deck.

Inside the cabin, Linette gave Maria a change of clothes and told her to stay out of sight as she felt the boat start to move away from the dock into the mainstream of the river. They needed to pass under more than ten bridges to get out of the city and the river snaked first southwest then almost northeast three times before they would be clear. They had an easterly breeze, so they could use sails, but it was a long way and would be slow going.

They had gotten as far as St. Dennis before they saw any signs of military or police activity. They could see riders racing down the roads heading west, and Marty knew that they would set up a barrage down-stream so they could search the boats.

It was nearly dark when they tied up at Argenteuil and made their way to a house on the Rue De la Liberte. Marty unlocked the door and let them in. It was owned by a sympathiser and was a safe house. Inside, it was stocked with food and changes of clothes for all of them. Luckily, the two girls were of similar build.

Marty went to a painting and lifted it from the wall. Behind it, was a hidden strong box, which he unlocked with a key he had on his keyring. Inside was money and false papers which would give them new identities. There were several sets of papers which they could fill in with new names. They decided that the best thing to do would be to split into two pairs; Marty with Maria and Linette with James and make their way to Amiens independently.

James and Linette chose to be brother and sister as they had enough in common to get away with it. Marty had a talk with Maria, and she agreed to pose as his wife. Linette suggested he needed to change his appearance, so he gave shaving a miss in the hope of growing a beard and Linette used theatrical makeup to darken his eyebrows and hair.

They laid low the next day and waited for their friend to visit with news. He arrived late that evening and told them that there was a general curfew at dusk, and no one was allowed to travel without special permission. He agreed their best course was to go via Amiens to Le Crotoy and use the smugglers to get them back to England. He promised he would be back the next morning with travel papers.

The next morning arrived, but their friend didn't show up. They had no option but to just wait.

It was mid-afternoon when he did arrive, and he was a little flustered.

"The Army have check points everywhere," he said, "the explosion at the house in Paris killed two policemen and hurt several more and they are blaming the Jacobins. They are also linking the bomb attack on Lucien Bonaparte to them as well. "

"Are they specifically linking them to us?" asked Marty.

"There is mention of two men that they are interested in questioning for this and the disappearance of a woman."

"No mention of a dog or another woman?"

"No, nothing like that."

"Then the plan stays as was," Marty concluded, "they aren't looking for two couples and its lucky I never took Blaez to the Ministry. Do you have the travel papers?"

The papers were laid out on the table. They were the standard form and had been signed by the Prefect of the district. Marty didn't ask how. All they had to do was fill in the names. The reasons for travel were to visit a dying relative in Amiens for Marty and Maria and to take over a farm from an elderly parent for James and Linette. They would have to get new documents once they got there.

Marty and Maria left at dawn the next day and hired a coach to take them to Amiens. They would stop overnight at Breteuil and change horses every twenty miles. James and Linette bought a single horse, dog cart and would take two days as well. But as the cart was open, it would be a far less comfortable journey.

As it turned out, the weather turned foul, and the coach kept getting bogged down on the badly kept roads. Marty had to help get it moving again. The dog cart being lighter didn't get stuck as much, but James and Linette were soaking wet, cold, and miserable by the time they arrived at the hotel run by a sympathiser in Amiens.

Marty and Maria turned up a day later having taken three days to get there. The good thing for both couples was that the weather was so bad that the police weren't at all attentive at the checkpoints, practically waving them through so as not to go out in the rain.

James donated the cart and horse to the hotel owner in payment for their rooms as they all needed to rest after that journey.

They stayed for three days then changed identity again. They also swapped partners to mix things up as well. Choosing new identities was a problem. Then Maria had an inspiration after visiting the cathedral. Now that Napoleon was in charge the church was no longer held in such disrespect and pilgrims were being seen again, they dressed and behaved as pilgrims from Le Crotoy who had walked to Amiens and were now returning home.

They started walking and had gotten about five kilometres outside of town when a friendly farmer gave them a ride in the back of his wagon. It had previously been used to transport hay so was clean, if a little hard on the backside.

Abbeville provided a refuge for the night in the form of a seedy hotel where the owner didn't ask questions. It was filthy, and they were all suffering from bed bug bites by the morning. They set out at false dawn. There had been a frost, so they set a good pace to stay warm. They reached Le Crotoy mid-afternoon. Marty left the others at a café and went with Blaez to make contact with the smugglers.

He returned after an hour and a half with Gaston, a smuggler he had dealings with before. He, in turn, led them to a safe house, provided changes of clothes and the raw materials for them to cook dinner.

All of them were lousy with vermin living on their bodies from the infested mattresses at the hotel. So, the boys rigged a private area screened off by blankets slung from the beams and boiled up plenty of water. They took it in turns to thoroughly wash themselves. The vermin ridden clothes were burnt.

Dinner was a generous fish stew with root vegetables cooked by the girls and fresh crusty bread covered in butter. They washed it down with a bottle of wine then settled around the fire. Marty thought that right at that minute life was good.

Word came the next morning that there wasn't a visit expected from the Deal Boys until after the new year. So, Marty entered into negotiation with the locals to have them sail them home. They knew they had him over a barrel. To start with were asking extortionate amounts of money for the service. Marty was working hard to try and talk them down. After a half an hour of keeping him on edge, they all suddenly burst out laughing and told him they were only joking.

*Funny bloody ha ha,* Marty thought but kept a smile on his face to show he could take a joke. They told him that if they could take a cargo of Brandy and bring back some English wool cloth, they would only charge him a little for the passengers. Marty knew the Deal boys would get drilled on the price of the Brandy, but it didn't matter as long as they got home.

Two weeks before Christmas, the four arrived in London by coach and made their way to William Wickham's home. Armand told him in Deal, that was where they would meet their masters, which was unusual. But then they hadn't had a hugely successful mission, so…

They were shown into the library once they arrived and had to wait until Wickham appeared. He was polite to Maria and immediately agreed to arrange for her to visit her husband. He then had her wait in his drawing room while he talked to the others.

"Well, what happened?" he asked in a cold voice. Marty gave his report as factually and without emotion as he could. Wickham cross-examined the others about details then sat back and regarded them with a steady stare.

"Well, I don't think I can blame you for putting Napoleon in the first consul's seat as it looks like sheer coincidence and bad luck. But we won't be running anymore missions in France until we can see what he will do next. Popular opinion has it that he will consolidate his position and may even sue for peace."

"What will happen to us?" Marty asked.

"Well, that is one reason we wanted this debriefing here rather than the Admiralty," Wickham replied, "The damn politicians will want to wind down the armed forces as soon as peace is agreed. The chance of a peace premium will put pressure on us to disband you and if we leave you in England and visible, the pressure will just mount. The First Sea Lord, Hood, and I, all want to keep the S.O.F. going." He paused as if considering what he would say next.

"Linette, would you join Madam St. Martin in the drawing room please?"

"Martin," he began as soon as she left.

# Chapter 10: A Brief Respite

Marty laid in the arms of his lover and contemplated his life to date. He had gone from cabin boy to lieutenant in five years. He had been in action or on duty the vast majority of that time but had still managed to meet and fall in love with Caroline. The fact that she waited for him while he was away, amazed him as did the depth of her passion when they got back together.

Later that day, they would go to a ball held by the Regent, and he would probably be presented to the King. The gossips had already noted his return and it would be common knowledge all over London society before he got there.

He also wanted to get down to Dorset to visit his family as he hadn't seen them since he was a midshipman. The good thing was he had time. He knew he wouldn't be sailing again until February - just before his 18th birthday.

At that moment, Caroline decided she needed his full and undivided attention, and the rest of the morning just flew by.


That evening, dressed in full dress uniform, he walked with Caroline on his arm through the doors of the ballroom at St. James palace. The herald announced in a loud voice,

"The Duchess of Candor and Lieutenant Stockley, Royal Navy"

Heads turned, and comments were whispered behind raised fans as they made their way across the floor. They were greeted by many of the good and the great in attendance. *Hypocrites,* thought Marty. He knew that both he and Caroline were thought of as 'new blood' that had 'no breeding'. 'All the same, he thought, she is a Baroness, and I am an officer, so they can stick that right up their…"

They joined the line to be presented to the Prince Regent and Caroline chatted merrily with the people to either side of them. He caught his first glimpse of the future King, and his first impression was, "What a dandy!" The Regent was resplendent in the latest fashion with his long hair styled to look a bit Navy-ish. He wore the symbols of his rank and other jewels and fairly glittered.

Suddenly, it was their turn, and Caroline elbowed him in the ribs to get his attention as she started to curtsey. Marty made a leg and bowed deeply as required.

"My dear Lady Caroline!" Prince George exclaimed as he kissed her proffered hand, "And this must be your dashing Lieutenant that all the ladies are talking about." He looked sideways at Admiral Hood, who was standing off to the side and added.

"I hear you are the protégé of that old fox, Hood. In and out of his office then disappearing to who knows where and getting blown up to boot!" He laughed.

Marty was taken aback and didn't know what to say when Hood materialized at his side and bowed to the prince.

"Your Highness," he said, "I see you have met one of our promising young officers." He made a point of glancing back along the line of people waiting to be introduced. "But I see you have quite the line of people waiting. I must not let him monopolise your time." And to Marty,

"Come, young man, you can't keep the prince all to yourself. There are other people waiting!" And led the bemused couple away. Marty glanced back and saw that the prince was watching them over the shoulder of the next person in line and grinning like a cat that just surprised a mouse.

Hood manoeuvred them to a quiet spot and said to Marty,

"That explains a number of things. We knew my office was being watched but didn't know who was behind it. That meddling fool doesn't know when to keep out of things he should leave alone."

"That explains the meeting at Wickham's house then," Marty observed.

"Yes, that is one debrief that we didn't want overheard," Hood replied

Caroline looked from one to the other and said,

"I think it's about time you two let me in on just what the hell you have been up to." She raised a hand to Hood before he could object and said, "Before you deny it, let me tell you I have sources of my own and have already guessed the truth about what goes on at the farm with the Deal boys. I am, after all, one of the biggest distributors of wine and spirits in England."

That was a complete surprise to Marty, who looked at her in astonishment.

"You think I just sit around and count my rent?" She laughed, "I am your 'Deal Boys' biggest customer."

Marty looked at Hood, who also looked surprised that a Lady was involved in trade, but got himself under control with an effort.

"They needed a network and money to distribute their 'imports'. I have access to my father's business network. It was quite simple to persuade him to allow me to use it to move my goods through it as well."

"Let's go for a walk through the long hall," Hood said.

The long hall was traditionally used by the ladies of the palace to exercise when the weather outside was inclement. It was quiet this evening and was lined with works of the world's most famous artists.

During their perambulation, Hood told Caroline about the true purpose of the farm and Marty's position as second in command. He didn't go into the details of their missions.

"You can see that it is vital that this is kept a secret for both the national interest and Martin's safety."

Caroline gave him one of her 'don't treat me like an idiot' looks and said,

"You have my word that I will not divulge this to another living soul."

"I never doubted it," smiled Hood

Slightly mollified she asked,

"Will the S.O.F. be kept going if Napoleon sues for peace?"

Hood barked a laugh and replied,

"If he does, it will just be so he can rebuild his forces, and we will need to be just as vigilant. But in the meantime, we need to scotch his ambitions elsewhere hence the S.O.F.'s next mission."

Marty decided that he need say nothing as the two of them were saying quite enough.

"The one starting in February," Caroline stated, and Hood nodded.

"How long will they be away?" She asked meaning 'he'.

"That depends on what they find and how fast they can carry out their orders," Hood replied.

"Not going into France?"

"My you are inquisitive! No, he won't be going back to France. His description is too well known right now."

Caroline finally looked satisfied. But then she stopped and looked Hood right in the eye.

"If you get him killed without having a damn good reason for what you ordered him to do, you WILL answer to me."

Hood smiled and said quietly and with absolute sincerity,

"My dear lady, if I did that, I would throw myself on my sword at your very feet."

The ball went well (he didn't end up getting into a duel) and they met up with the de Marchet family. He had to break the news that he would be away for Evelyn's spring wedding. The Count was, as usual, accepting. Evelyn, cross at first then forgiving and the countess, concerned. He told her he would have time to heal properly this time, and that seemed to make things better for her.

He was surprised at the number of women who wanted to make his acquaintance. Caroline was imperious and made it abundantly clear that God had better help any woman that stepped over the mark, because her retribution would be biblical!

All this, of course, played right into the hands of the gossips who were speculating in the next day's papers when the two would tie the knot! Marty groaned as he read that over breakfast the next morning and looked at Caroline across the table and asked,

"When do we leave London?"

She laughed and said, "We can leave for Dorset after the Duke of York's Christmas Ball on Friday. Why? Is London society getting to you?"

"I feel like a prize bull being examined by every snooping ninny in the city. Listen to this, 'Our gallant Lieutenant was dressed in his finest uniform, the tight breeches of which did nothing to hide the manliness that the ladies are finding maddening.' I mean, is nothing sacrosanct!"

Caroline looked archly across at him and said,

"Well, what do you think got my attention to start with?" and then laughed delightedly as he blushed furiously.

# Chapter 11: Surprise Surprise!

Saturday found them in a coach, well-wrapped in blankets and heading to Dorset. They stayed in the usual Inns and arrived on Monday sixteenth December in Wareham. They took rooms in the Red Lion as they did before and got a good night's rest before heading over the bridge to Stoborough.

Marty got the driver to stop by the school and walked over to the door. The windows were bright with candlelight, and he could see children at their desks through the dusty glass.

He opened the door and walked in. It was just as he remembered it the last time he was there six years before. The desks looked tiny, but the slates, chalk and Miss Turner stood at the front hadn't changed.

Katy Turner looked over her shoulder as the door opened and saw a handsome young man in expensive clothes stood there. It took her a second to recognise him then she exclaimed,

"Marty! Come in! Come in! Children, this is Marty Stockley, the brother of Helen."

Marty looked around the expectant faces and said,

"Good morning. I am pleased to see you all,"

A particularly grubby urchin looked at him and squawked,

"'e aint 'elen's brover! He be in the Navy and this un speaks funny like you miss, an' he aint carryin' that big knife that Marty does."

Marty crouched down so he was face to face with the little tyke, pulled his knife from its sheath, and set it point down on his desk.

"Be this wha' yer lookin' fer," he said in his best Dorset dialect to the now wide-eyed boy and a chorus of "Coo's! and Cor's! from the rest of the class.

A giggle from behind alerted him to the fact that Caroline had crept in behind him.

"Why don't you tell them how you met Blaez?" she said as the dog pushed himself under Marty's arm, put out he wasn't the centre of attention.

"Cor, a proper lady!" a little girl blurted out, making Marty laugh.

Marty settled down with the class all around him and told a heavily edited version of the adventure in Holland. Blaez played his part by letting the children pet him and rolling on his back so they could scratch his tummy. At the end, he stood and embraced Miss Katy and asked,

"Is Helen teaching?"

"She helps out two days a week. I'm getting a little old to do this full time," Katy replied. "She is at the house with your mother today."


They pulled up at the house, and it was quiet. Marty knocked on the door, pushed it open, and yelled "Hellooo." Blaez pushed his way past and headed straight for the kitchen as his sister Helen exploded out of the door and jumped into his arms.

"I knew you would be 'ere for Christmas bruv!"

Sister Jane appeared and went straight to Caroline and gave her a big hug.

"Is Arthur here?" Marty asked.

"He'll be by later after he be done at the forge," Helen told him.

Marty looked at Jane and noticed the slight swelling of her stomach and grinned at her.

"So, Stephen Barnes has finally got around to getting you pregnant," he observed. Jane had married the oldest Barnes boy the year before.

"That he has," she grinned, "We be just waiting for Nick Hayball to do the same for 'elen."

"We be workin' on it!" Helen retorted in a slightly offended voice. She had only gotten married two months ago.

"Mum be in the parlour with Grandad," Jane told him, a hint he should get a move on.

Marty walked into the house and went through to the Parlour. His mother sat with his grandfather by the fire, and she looked up at him as he walked in.

"Oh my! Dad look at our Marty! He be a proper gentleman now."

She stood, and he took her in his arms and gave her a long hug. His grandfather tried to stand, but Marty made him stay seated and leant down to give him a hug too.

"What ever happened to yer hair?" his mother exclaimed as he bent over, and she got a good view of the back of his head.

"Long story, Mum. I'll tell you all later." He laughed.

"You've grown, boy," his grandfather observed a bit unnecessarily.

"Ay, that be Navy food, Pop." He smiled back at him.

His mother noticed Caroline stood in the doorway and went to greet her but stopped halfway and put her hand to her mouth and said,

"Oh my!"

Marty looked at her puzzled.

Caroline smiled and nodded then the two women were in each other's arms, tears streaming down their faces. Now Marty was totally confused and didn't know what the hell was going on.

His mother looked over her shoulder at him and said to Caroline,

"You aint told 'im yet?"

Caroline shook her head.

"Told me what?" Marty asked, still totally unknowing.

Caroline went to him and took his hands in hers and with tears still in her eyes said,

"You are going to be a father, Martin. I'm pregnant."

He almost fell over.

"What?" he said in a tiny voice.

"I'm Pregnant," she said again.

"Oh, my Lord!" He crowed, "I'm going to be a father?"

She nodded almost shyly.

He picked her up and swung her around then stopped and looking concerned, put her gently down.

"It's alright, I won't break, and neither will the baby," she laughed.

He looked at her and asked the question all first-time fathers ask,

"How, I mean when?"

"The blindfold," she replied enigmatically.

Marty blushed bright red as his mother looked at him quizzically.

"Never mind," he told her, "It were about two months ago."

He suddenly looked as if he had an epiphany.

"We have to get married!"

He dropped to his knee in front of Caroline and took her hands in his. He looked up at her beseechingly and said,

"Caroline, I know I am but a poor lieutenant in His Majesty's Navy, but I have prospects and can care for you in the way you should be. Will you consent to be my wife and partner for life?"

Caroline beamed at him with such a smile he thought it would blind him and said,

"Oh yes I do, with all my heart!"

Then all hell broke loose as his sisters descended on Caroline and his grandfather and his brother, Arthur, who had just arrived, took him by the hand and shook it, congratulating him.

His mother finally got to grab him and hold him tight.

"She be the one for you," she said, "I knew it the first time I saw her."

After that, the day descended into a round of congratulations from visitors as messages were sent to the rest of his brothers and sisters and other relatives that lived nearby.


That evening back at the Red Lion, they sat in their room too tired to do much else than just chat in front of the fire.

"We will have to have the bans read soon so we can marry before I leave on the next mission," Marty said, "I don't want to go, but I have my duty."

"Of course, you must go!" Caroline replied forcibly. "You are a sailor, and I will be a sailor's wife. I know what I am joining up to!"

"But I want to be here for when it's born."

"If you are, it will be fantastic, but if you are away, it will still be alright."

She moved over to him, sat on his lap, took his hand, and placed it on her heart.

"You will be here with me whatever happens. But the more immediate problem is where will we hold the wedding ceremony?"

"Oh, I hadn't thought about that. If we do it here, your family have to travel down, but if we do it in Cheshire, then I will have to ship all of mine up there."

"Well, it's obvious, isn't it?" Caroline said.

"We do it in London. It's around halfway between the two families, and we can have all your Navy friends along as well."

Marty groaned.

"Can you see my family mixing with all your relatives?"

"Oh, I'm sure mine will cope." She smiled. "They won't be able to understand a word they say anyway." She then dissolved into giggles as Marty tickled her in revenge for that remark.

Over the next week, messengers were flying in and out of Wareham as instructions were sent to the church for the banns to be read, announcements made in newspapers and family and friends informed. They left for London on the twenty-seventh of December.

As soon as they arrived at the house, they were immediately inundated with visitors bringing congratulations, but mostly just to be nosey. The exceptions were the de Marchet's, Hood, and Armand. They came just to let the happy couple know that they had their support and love. Even Evelyn was happy and when let in on the secret of the baby, got over her snit at them getting married before she did.

The big surprise was a discrete visit from William Wickham. He sat with the two of them, gave them his blessing, and surprised Marty by saying,

"You had better get used to the idea that you will be the new Baron Candor and how you will handle that young man. Oh, and please do not forget that you have to invite the King and Prince Regent to the ceremony."

Marty looked at him in absolute horror. This part of their union hadn't even entered his mind!

"But how? Baronies aren't usually passed on through marriage. The King at the wedding?" he stammered.

"They don't want the Candor Barony to expire so made an exception for you. It's all to do with the lands you will soon own and you being a member of parliament. As for the wedding, it's traditional," Wickham replied, "Mind you, he has his good days and bad days, so he probably won't show up at all."

Marty knew the king had a problem with his mind and was often so unstable that he often couldn't be seen in public.

"He has to approve the marriage as it now involves a Barony. But I have it on good authority that in a lucid moment, he has already signed the permission."

"What?" said Marty, "But I haven't asked for it."

Wickham looked smug and said,

"Well, I took the liberty of sending a letter of request in your name. Thought it would save time."

Marty was so shocked he could say nothing.

Two days later, they found that it was true when a royal messenger delivered a packet with the royal seal containing the official document.

Because of the rush to get married before he left and before Caroline was showing her pregnancy too much, the ceremony would be smaller than her status would normally warrant. But even so, it would be far from a cosy family affair and Caroline employed a veritable army of people to organise it.

This all culminated in Marty being driven to St Martin-in-the-fields in a carriage accompanied by Armand and the Count de Marchet. It was mid-February, and he had been staying with the count and his family for the last two weeks.

He was dressed in uniform and wore the dress sword that Caroline had given him. His knees were weak, and he was sweating despite the cold. He wondered if he was getting a fever but, it was just his nerves.

They arrived at the church, and he was escorted in by the count acting instead of his father and Armand who was his best man.

His family had all been coached up to London and taken under the wing of the countess, who acted like an aunt to all of them. She took his sisters and his brother's wives out and got them dresses and Evelyn's fiancé, Arthur, got the men suited and booted.

As he entered, he was amazed to see not just his family on his side of the church but most of the boys from the farm: Bill Clarence, his wife, brother, and son as well. Admiral Hood was also there with the First Sea Lord, and Marty thought he caught a glimpse of Wickham in the shadows.

On Caroline's side, he saw Captains Coburn, Pellew, and Admiral Nelson. That surprised him as he had no idea there was any kind of link with him and Caroline's family. He found out later the link with Nelson was with Lady Hamilton, who was a friend of Caroline's mother. She was also there.

Captain Turner and the officers of the Falcon couldn't attend as they were at sea, but Katy came and that made up for it somewhat.

He had been standing near the alter for what felt like an age when he sensed her presence. He looked around and saw her walking up the isle on the arm of her father with Evelyn in attendance as maid of honour and several young girl relatives as bridesmaids. But it was Caroline that dominated his vision. Dressed in a traditional red dress, she stunned him with her beauty and the rest of the ceremony passed in a blur. He remembered mumbling 'I do' a couple of times but that was about it. The next thing he knew, he was walking down the aisle with Caroline on his arm. As they exited the church, they walked under an arch of oars held by the crew of the Snipe.

The wedding party was at her, no, their London house and the mix of dialects on show was amazing. Yorkshire from Caroline's family, Dorset from his, Norfolk from Nelson and Kent from Pelew.

The king hadn't made an appearance, but the prince Regent did. Marty hadn't seen him in the church as he was up in a gallery, away from the hoi polloi. He came to the house but left after greeting the bride and groom, giving them his blessing and a present of matching diamond studded brooches with their coats of arms on.

What Marty couldn't get used to was being addressed as 'my Lord.' Apparently, he was conferred the title as soon as he said, 'I do.' The king's advisors figured it was better to keep it simple rather than risk any kind of public demonstration of his majesty's infirmity and so wrapped up the barony with the wedding permission. His sisters were loving it, of course. His mother just accepted it all calmly and basked in his reflected glory.

He was brought down to earth with a bump a week later when his orders arrived for his next mission.

# Chapter 12: Crossing the Line

Two days before his 18th Birthday Lieutenant, Lord Candor, otherwise known as Lieutenant Stockley, stood on the quarter-deck of his ship, the Snipe, and navigated her out of the river Stour into the English Channel. After a talk with Admiral Hood, he had decided not to use his title in the service. First off, he didn't feel comfortable wearing it yet and, second, he knew it would just cause resentment from other officers. So, on ship, he was just plain Lieutenant Stockley.

His wedding to Caroline had been on the front page of every newspaper in Britain. They even had artist's impressions of the ceremony, which were largely fantasy as no one from the press was allowed into the church or the party afterwards. He had wondered if his new-found celebrity and status would disqualify him from working with the S.O.F. but Wickham had just scoffed and said it was a storm in a teacup and everyone would forget it soon enough. In any case, he added with a smirk, all the drawings showed him to be taller and more handsome than he was in real life so no one would recognise him.

The Snipe had been completely refit. She had new copper on her bottom and a new mast. The old mast had been nibbled at by a French lugger and was deemed inadequate for the trip they were undertaking. She also had all new rigging and the carronades fitted with the latest design carriages. She looked and handled like a new craft.

They were on a mission to Madagascar. Intelligence had it that the French were sponsoring the pirates out of there to attack British merchant shipping. It was being done in such a way that is made it hard to attribute it directly to the French. Napoleon was also making noises that he wanted peace and the politicians were terrified to do anything that might upset that. So, the S.O.F. got the job of either finding proof or scotching the piracy at source.

Consequently, the Snipe and her big sister, the Sloop Alouette, were now making sail south down the channel with full Navy crews. In fact, there were still several Deal boys on the roster, but they had been signed up as volunteers and now counted as Navy.

The plan was to sail down to the cape then reconnoitre Madagascar, the surrounding islands and African coast, see where the pirate bases were, then posing as French privateers infiltrate them and try and make the connection with French government sponsorship. Whether they made the connection or not, they were to either destroy those bases or come up with a plan where they could be destroyed with the help of local Navy assets.

Once they had done all that, they could go home.

Marty was down in his cabin putting away the extra things that Caroline had made him take with him. Included was a sash with the emblems of his barony pinned to it in case he had to attend a formal function. That got put in the bottom of his chest wrapped in tissue paper. There was also a portrait of her, which he put on the wall of his cabin where he could see it when he was at his desk. Other items were stowed in his desk or in the small dresser.

She also had delivered a ton of personal stores from London, including bottled preserves, jars of butter, hams, bacon, rounds of cheese, jam and a host of dried and salted foods.

They had a new surgeon's mate on the Snipe to go with a new Surgeon on the Alouette. These gentlemen were also onboard as a result of Caroline's intervention.

Blaez was curled up on his blanket and was sporting a rather savage-looking spiked collar that Marty's brother Arthur had made him. Arthur was now a fully qualified Smith and had his own forge thanks to Marty's sponsorship. Marty was quietly setting up all his siblings and their families in new businesses to get them away from the mines, and he had plans to buy farms in the Purbeck area and run them in a much more modern way. But first, he needed to get this mission done.

His birthday came around for the eighteenth time, and he celebrated it by giving the crew a double rum ration and having a celebratory dinner with his midshipman, cox, and quartermaster. There wasn't enough room in his cabin for anymore, so he donated some of his personal stores to making sure the crew had a good meal as well.

They sailed South, or as close as they could with the prevailing winds, passed the straits of Heracles, and down to the coast of Morocco. They continued down to the Portuguese island of Cape Verde where they re-watered and stocked up on fruit and vegetables. Marty and Armand were disgusted by the evidence of slave trading that they saw. The islands had been a staging point for slavers for years and nothing had changed.

Marty was intrigued by the changes in the climate and the way the clouds formed and changed over the day. He made extensive notes on every aspect of the voyage so he could use them on later ones. He also wrote about them in extended sea letters to his wife, mother, the De Marchets and Miss Kate.

The days dragged on, and Marty started teaching some of the hands who wanted to learn to read and write. Midshipman Campbell joined in and soon they had quite a school going. For those that didn't want to learn to read or didn't feel able to learn, he would sit in the evenings on the capstan and read to them from a collection of books he had brought with him.

He didn't know it, but he was bonding his crew to him in a way that most captains never did. They respected him and would follow him to hell and back if he asked them without even asking why. His hard-core team of the four Basques, Wilson, Tom, and John Smith were always there ready to help, care for Blaez (and clean up after him) and keep the rest of crew in line. They were his unofficial enforcers, and everybody knew it.

They approached the equator. As was traditional, the old salts who'd crossed it before asked permission to honour Neptune and celebrate the crossing by initiating the first timers. Marty said yes then realised he was a potential initiate as well.

What can only be described as a canvas lined pool was erected on deck and filled with sea water. At one end, a throne was made from spare wood and decorated with seaweed and seashells. (The Lord only knew where they got the shells). A platform was erected opposite the throne and also decorated. Several covered buckets were placed around it.

On the day they crossed the line, Tom Savage appeared dressed as Neptune in a toga made from material scrounged from the slops store, seaweed wig and a large triton. He was escorted by four handmaidens, who were the Basques dressed as girls with seaweed wigs. In a loud and commanding voice, he announced,

"Hear ye all! For tis I, lord Neptune, king of the sea, come to collect my tribute from those virgins who aint crossed the line afore." – A roar from the crew - "My beautiful handmaidens!" – cat calls and whistles – "Bring forth the initiates!" A half a dozen men were brought forward all naked apart from a loincloth and pushed forward onto the platform. With a start, Marty recognised James Campbell and wondered how the hell they had talked him into this.

The first of the initiates was led to the front of the platform by two of the handmaidens. He was restrained and the third dipped into a bucket that they could now see was full of mush, fat from the boiled beef. He liberally smeared the victim with the foul-smelling grease then delved in another bucket and smeared him with soot.

The next victim was pushed forward, it was James. He was grabbed and greased, but this time they grabbed a handfuls of feathers from a third bucket and he had them poured over him. The other two fared no better.

When they were all suitably covered, Tom stood, shook his Trident in the air, and roared.

"Pay homage to the king of the ocean, you swabs!"

His handmaidens knocked out the forward supports to the platform allowing it to tip forward and dunk the initiates in the water. That was the signal for the rest of the crew to pelt them with wet rags and buckets of water.

Marty let the mayhem continue for a few minutes and watched it spread across the deck until almost everyone had received a soaking. Blaez was watching beside him and was barking furiously at the fun.

He decided enough was enough and signalled to Tom to put a stop to it just as a badly aimed bucket of water caught him full in the chest. The thrower stood with his mouth agape and looked as if he wished the sea would swallow him up! But Marty just grinned and pushed him into the pool.

Tom had a hard time yelling for order because he was laughing fit to bust a rib.

Blaez sat beside Marty looking bemused as half the water had hit him too.

Finally, order was restored. Marty quietly 'requested' that they put his ship back into order and then went to his cabin to get a change of clothes.

Once past the equator, they steered Southeast to make landfall somewhere on the West coast just North of the Cape. They got lucky and didn't find the doldrums, but they did experience some truly huge rollers that had the whole of the Atlantic to build up.

They made landfall and turned south to follow the coast. They had long before run out of fresh food and were digging into the salt beef and pork stowed deep in the hold supplemented by lime juice laced into their rum ration.

Cape Town was held by the British in 1800 and was a safe place to launch their campaign in Madagascar. They arrived in the middle of May after being at sea for 10 weeks. The crew and ships were tired and needed a break. They dropped anchor in the bay in the lee of Robin Island while they waited for a pilot to bring them into the docks.

When they finally moored, Armand and Marty went ashore to pay their respects to the Port Admiral. Vice Admiral Sir Roger Curtis was deeply embittered by his perceived exile to Cape Town and when two young officers were shown into his office and one of them was obviously French, his temper flared.

"Your credentials had better be bloody perfect or I will have you in my brig faster than you can say Bonaparte," he growled.

Armand handed over his orders and a letter from the first sea lord and waited.

Sir Roger read the orders and then the letter and looked at Armand then at Marty.

"Lord Candor?"

Marty winced and replied, "Aye, sir. But I prefer plain Lieutenant Stockley."

He kept his eyes straight ahead aware that Sir Roger outranked him in the Navy but now knew he was outranked socially. Not what Marty wanted.

"Working undercover, posing as privateers, secret missions? Whose Navy do you work for?"

"That is secret and, on a need-to-know basis only," said Armand.

Sir Roger looked them over one more time, tempted to rip into Armand for that comment but then thinking that if these two had the ear of the first sea lord...

"Take a seat and tell me what you need," he said.

# Chapter 13: The Madagascar Caper

They took a few days to rest the men and get both ships into first class condition again. They took on as many fresh stores as they could and cleaned and refilled all of their water barrels.

Marty and Armand sent the men into the town to get some shore leaves and to try and gather any information about piracy in the area that they could find. It turned out to be not much. So, as soon as they could, they set off again.

There wasn't much between Cape Town and Madagascar in terms of settlements. In fact, most of the East coast wasn't even surveyed properly. So, they decided to take a cruise and see what they could find.

It took ten days to sail into the straits between Madagascar and the mainland. They found a bay with good shelter and fresh water at around the same latitude as the southern end of the island. It showed signs of being used by someone as there were old fire pits and piles of bones from something that looked a bit like a deer. It was as good a base as any, so they set up camp there.

Marty took the snipe and started scouting up the coast, and Armand went to have a look at Madagascar.


The Snipe was making good time as she cruised North. They had investigated every inlet and bay but saw nothing of interest. Then as the coast swung Northeast, they came upon a chain of islets with a long golden beach behind on the mainland.

Marty reduced sail and took his time. He wanted the leisure to look at every one and mark them on his growing map. They eventually came up on an inlet that looked like the entrance was protected by a sandbar running from the Southern edge to the Northeast. A Natural harbour. Marty steered them in closer and had two men in the bow checking the depth with lead lines.

They felt their way up to the sand bar and ran along it until they could see into the inlet to the Northwest. There, sat on a promontory between what could be two rivers, was a village and moored up around it were around a dozen sleek looking, single masted boats. *Dhows,* Marty thought.

Marty had the French flag run up and they hove-to. He told the men to arm themselves and look privateer-ish. It didn't take long for one of the boats by the village to be crewed and start out.

Marty watched them come through a telescope and noted that while most of the crew were half-naked black natives, there were two men at the stern who looked more like the men he had seen in North Africa. They were dressed in flowing robes and were lighter skinned.

On a whim, he had a canvas chair set up on the quarterdeck under the awning they had set to protect the helmsman from the sun. He ordered the carronades covered as he wanted their strength concealed.

The boat came up to their side, and the two Arabic men stepped up on the deck. Marty set two of his men to study the boat, its rigging, any armament, and capacity. One was a fair sketch and would make drawings for later reference.

Marty received the men lounging in his chair with Blaez next to him. He was armed with his knife and Campbell's sabre as it looked more impressive than his hanger.

The two men were dressed in black robes cinched at the waist by a sash, from which hung long curved, richly decorated knives on one side and large curved swords with wide blades on the other. Their heads were covered in a cloth that wrapped around in such a way as to leave a loop below the chin.

Marty studied them as they approached. The smaller one had a pocked-marked face with a prominent hooked nose. The other had darker skin, an almost equine nose, long and straight, and high cheekbones.

They stopped in front of him and touched their right hands to their hearts, mouths, and foreheads in some kind of salute. Marty nodded back and said in French,

"I am Cecile De Borcey, Captain of this ship, and you are?"

The smaller of the two said in perfect French,

"Ahmed Bahri, and my associate is Fahd Kamara. We are his eminence, the Sultan of Morocco's, representatives in this area."

*That's interesting,* Marty thought as he knew Morocco was a French Colony.

"Then I am pleased if you are able to pass my respects and greetings to his highness," Marty replied.

"We are intrigued as to what the purpose of your visit is, Captain? We were not expecting a visit from a representative of the French Government at this time."

Marty took that in and interpreted it as they were expecting a visit later. He decided to stir things up.

"Oh, I am not from the government. They are in confusion since Napoleon Bonaparte took over and are still running around like headless chickens."

He saw a flicker of – something – in Ahmed's face. Surprise?

"So, what is your mission here?" Fahd asked.

"We are privateers," Marty stated, "We have come to try our luck against the Roast-beef's East India men. We have a letter of marque from the French Ministry giving us permission to operate in this area."

*Hook cast,* Marty thought.

There was no mistaking the look of anger that passed over both men's faces at that.

*Bait taken.*

"But eminent Captain, we have an agreement with the Government for exclusive…" started Ahmed before Fahd grabbed his arm and drew him away.

I bet he was going to say exclusive rights, thought Marty.

They came back, and Ahmed looked calmer.

"We have an agreement with the Revolutionary Government of France with respect to defending their interest in this area," he stated.

"Ahh, I see the problem then," Marty sighed almost in regret. "The revolutionary government is no longer in charge. Napoleon is now in command. The revolution is over." He pointed at them. "Your agreement is no longer valid!"

*Let's see how you like that!* He thought.

The two of them had a heated exchange in some other language then both turned to Marty and touched their heart, mouths, and head and Fahd said,

"We will verify what you say with our master. May we offer you the hospitality of our humble village while we wait for an answer?"

*Oh no you don't!* Marty smiled inwardly. *I wasn't born yesterday!*

"I would normally jump at the chance," he smiled, then held out his hands in a 'what can I do?' gesture and added, "but I have information that the illustrious East India Company has ships coming this way soon, and I intend to make some money while I can. Now, I am sure I have detained you long enough," he said in dismissal.

The two men genuflected again and turned away, still talking rapidly in that foreign language, and as soon as their boat cleared the side, he made the order to get under way. He ordered all plain sail as he figured this wouldn't be a healthy place for much longer.

They sailed West until they dropped below the horizon then turned to the south to make their way back to base.


Marty was at their base camp for two days before Armand arrived. They got together on the beach at sunset and discussed what they had found.

Armand had identified the main port where the pirates were operating from and contacted the locals. He was just about to leave when a dhow had come racing into the harbour. They had stuck around to see what had happened. It didn't take long when a horde of men had boiled out of the town, boarded boats, and started towards them.

To say the least, they got the hell out of there as fast as they could.

Marty told him of their encounter and his conversation with the 'emissaries'.

"You stirred up the bee's nest," stated Armand.

"Hornet's nest," Marty corrected him.

"It looks like they haven't had any contact with the French government for some time," he added, "Our arrival and that bluff have shaken things up a treat!"

"Yes, my young friend, your instinct for making trouble has paid dividends, and now we need to make things even more chaotic."

"What do you have in mind," Marty asked.


Two days later, the two ships were running North towards the inlet where Marty had met the emissaries of the Sultan. They were hoping the pirates would come out and they could surprise them with their firepower, so they made no attempt to conceal themselves and flew the French Tricolour from their masts.

"Loud and Proud." as Marty put it.

He had his crew relaxing, but nobody was fooled, they all knew that all hell could break loose at any time. All their weapons were in prime condition despite the damp atmosphere. Not a spot of rust on a blade or in a barrel. Marty had checked every man, and he knew they were as ready for a fight as they could be. A couple were below being treated for sickness, but it wasn't anything that frightened the surgeon's mate, so he was confident they were ready for anything.

As they approached the chain of islets, the lookouts on the Alouette could be heard hailing the deck. A couple of minutes later. his own lookouts were calling down.

"DECK THERE! A WHOLE LOAD OF SAIL DEAD AHEAD."

Marty had expected that they would face all twelve boats that they had seen around the village. But when he went up the rat lines to look for himself, he got a bit of a shock! There must have been twenty from the fast Dhows that he had seen to a couple of big Xebecs. They were in for the fight of their lives!

He knew that Armand would go after the Xebecs as he had the firepower to take them down. He would have to try and use the cutters manoeuvrability and enormous firepower to keep the smaller Dhows off his back.

"Load all carronades with double ball. Reload with that until we are within a cable then canister over ball," he ordered, "You will have to load as fast as you can and keep those bastards from boarding us."

He looked to his marines.

"Get every swivel we have and load them with grape. Keep them firing at anything within pistol shot. Concentrate your fire on the crews forget the hulls."

He looked down his deck at the confident look on their faces. Even the ships boys had an attitude that spoke of confidence and faith in him. He swallowed and looked from face to face, fixing them in his mind.

"You are my men, and I will not let you down. Now, let's get to it and murder those bastards!"

He ordered the tiller over, so they separated from the Alouette to Larboard. He kept on that tack until he was heading to the most landward edge of the approaching fleet. He knew Armand was edging over toward the seaward edge. At a range of four cables, he swung around to starboard to run along the line of the approaching ships.

"FIRE AS YOU BEAR," he yelled, and the carronades coughed and jerked back on their slides. The routine set in.

Reload – Fire – Reload - Fire – Reload - Fire.

Damn, they were firing at better than two rounds every minute and a half!

"Cannister over Ball!"

Fire – Reload – Fire – Reload

He could see the Alouette, smoke belching from her guns as she raked the line of ships on the opposite tack. Then he saw her turn to take on the biggest of the Xebecs.

"We will cross her stern and take out any boats that try to get behind her," he told John Smith, who was at the wheel.

He looked behind and was gratified that they had evened the odds a bit. He could see at least half a dozen boats that weren't going anywhere except down to Neptune's locker. But there were still plenty of boats to worry about and a couple were working their way around to get behind him. He would worry about them when they got closer

There were three that he was concerned about as they were racing in towards the Alouette. He changed course to run between them and his friends. Armand must have seen them too, and he fired off his long guns on that side when the pirates were five hundred yards away damaging one but not stopping it. He saw the Lark approaching and waved to Marty before turning his attention back to the Xebec that was almost in range.

Marty swung across his stern just in time as the other two Dhows were swinging into line. That's when he realised that some had cannon mounted. It was hard to miss the puffs of smoke and the shriek of shot across the deck.

His gunners responded without orders. They knew what to do and made sure they aimed well. At least two of the carronades must have aimed for the nearest Dhow as it just disintegrated in a cloud of shattered wood. The second staggered and swerved away as it was hit by a storm of cannister.

He looked around and realised the two that had been working their way around behind him were only a couple of hundred yards away and closing fast.

He yelled to tack and swung the ship to larboard. He made it halfway and the wind dropped!

The turn continued under their momentum, but it wouldn't be enough to bring the guns to bear.

The Alouette was exchanging broadsides with the xebec. Well, he could damn well help her! As his guns swung across the big pirate ship, he ordered the crews to give her one for the boys!

Blaez's barking brought his attention back to the other Dhows. One was almost up to them. They had sweeps and were rowing themselves into board.

"Swivels to the stern!" He called, and the marines responded immediately. Four of the nasty little guns were quickly mounted and fired, dealing a load of death at the crews of the approaching boats. He heard a couple of the carronades fire again then there was a grating noise as a Dhow ran along side.

A head appeared over the rail and a seaman shot it at point-blank range with a pistol. The head exploded and disappeared only to be replaced with half a dozen more. Marty yelled and ran into the attack. Shooting his pistols on the move and taking out a couple more. Then he was in amongst them as they poured up the side. He went to work with frantic ferocity. Either side of him were Tom and the Basques. Blaez was savaging any pirate that got past them. Marty staggered as a pirate got in a lucky thrust that ran across his ribs.

He smashed the sword away with his hanger and was about to thrust with his knife when both the man's hands were hacked off by James Campbells sabre.

He didn't have time to thank him as James kicked the handless man in the chest sending him over the side and turned to take on another screaming savage.

The boat rocked, and he felt wind on his cheek. It gusted stronger and the cutter started moving away from the boarders' boat.

They boys finished off the last of the boarders and Marty took stock of what was going on. The Alouette was winning the fight with the Xebec, which had large shot holes at her waterline and was sinking. It looked to Marty as if there were still around half the Dhows left and the other Xebec. Armand looked as if he was preparing to move on and take on another target. He wouldn't have to go far as the pirates were closing in on them.

He guessed that they had about ten minutes respite before it all started again. He moved around the crew checking who was hurt and if they needed treatment or could go on fighting. He ordered all pistols and swivels reloaded.

The surgeon's mate stopped him and made him take off his shirt so he could check his wound. Marty was surprised to see the gash in his skin and then remembered the sting as something had hit him. He got the mate to just pour raw spirit on it to cleanse it and to wrap a bandage around his chest.

He had lost two men so far. One of them was the Basque, Pablo, who had taken on three pirates and killed two before the third stabbed him in the side. The other was one of the new men that had joined just for this mission. He would mourn both later. The rest were walking wounded, and all said they could fight on.

Blaez was fine and had blood all over his face but none of it his. Tom had a cut or two and the other three Basques were unhurt but very angry over the death of Pablo.

He ordered the deck cleared of bodies and the dead pirates were thrown overboard. Just then, a huge grey and white shape launched itself out of the water, catching a body in its gaping maw. It was the biggest shark any of them had ever seen and must have been twenty feet long!

Marty looked over the side and saw that there were dozens of the big grey shapes under the water. Then the screams started from the ships that were wrecked as the survivors came face to face with their worst nightmare.

He had no time to worry about them as the other Dhows were closing in. He called the men to action again.

He noticed the three remaining Basques had separated, one to either beam amidships and Matai at the bow. Then Matai threw back his head and gave out a cry that started slowly and got faster to its climax.

"Eye, Yiy, Yiy, Yiy, Yiy, Yiy, Yiy, Yiy, Yiy Yeeehhhaaa!" echoed across the water.

It was answered by Antton.

"Eye, Yiy, Yiy, Yiy, Yiy, Yiy, Yiy, Yiy, Yiy Yeeehhhaaa, Yiy!"

Then Garai.

"Eye, Yiy, Yiy, Yiy, Yiy, Yiy, Yiy, Yiy, Yiy Yeeehhhaaa! Eye, Yiy."

The sound was earie and compelling and strangely uplifting.

Then the whole crew stood and shook their weapons in the air and screamed their defiance at the approaching craft.

"Eye, Yiy, Yiy, Yiy, Yiy, Yiy, Yiy, Yiy, Yiy Yeeehhhaaa!"

They finished with a cheer as the Lark ploughed between two Dhows, and the carronades on both sides roared their battle cry.

The fight got down and dirty from then on. Marty sailed his ship to cover the stern of the Alouette and they fought like daemons. The carronades became too hot to touch, and they had to swab them extra carefully to avoid premature detonation of the charges. They ran out of cannister and were loading chain and langridge instead.

It seemed to go on forever, and Marty's arms were leaden from swinging his sword. But then, suddenly, it was over. No more screaming pirates were trying to board, the carronades had nothing to shoot at, the swivels were silent.

He stood, and Blaez nuzzled his hand. He automatically reached down to rub his head as he looked around at the absolute carnage. He was too numb to feel appalled at the scene before him.

The deck was stacked three or four deep around the rail with dead pirates. *They look like a wall,* he thought. The sea around them was covered in wreckage and floating bodies. The sharks weren't feeding anymore. They'd had their fill.

He looked at the Alouette and saw Armand stood at the rail. He waved, and Armand waved back ' then beckoned for them to sail up alongside.

Marty didn't need to tell the crew to clean up the ship. James was already organising the men into parties and the dead were being dumped overboard, or, if they were their own, laid out amidships. Marty noticed that James was limping and had a bloody stain on his right leg.

John Smith was still at the wheel and Marty checked he was alright as there were more than a few dead bodies around him.

"I be fine, sir. Just had to take care of these few unwanted visitors."

Marty counted at least ten bodies and wondered at the man who could kill that many and still steer the ship. The giant Wilson was leaning on the rail just staring out to sea then shook himself, nodded to Marty and started throwing the bodies over the side.

They used the deck pump to wash the gore from both the ship and themselves, then buried their dead at sea well away from the battle to be clear of the sharks. Both crews had lost men but for Marty the loss of Pablo was particularly hard.

He asked Matai what the call meant that he had made. He explained that in the mountains, they would communicate with those calls and the one he made was a farewell to a friend and a promise of revenge.

Two days later Marty, Armand and their two midshipmen sat on the beach at their impromptu base eating a meal of some deer-like animal a couple of the marines had shot. The crew were either lazing around or playing an impromptu game of cricket. They had already had their lunch.

"So, the two Xebecs came from Madagascar," Ryan Thompson said, "Does that mean that all those extra Dhows came from there as well?"

"Probably," Armand said, "But we won't know for sure unless we have a look."

"Why did they attack us en-masse?" James pondered out loud.

"We are a threat to their operation and would cut into their profits. I believe Marty's comments triggered a, how you say, field war," Armand said.

"Turf war," Marty said automatically "Armand is right. They think we are here to take over the piracy business and they obviously don't like that."

"When will we go to take a look?" Thompson said.

"Well, we need to restock with powder and shot first," Marty observed, "We damn near emptied the magazine of everything in the last fight."

"Yes, and our gunners need a rest. They almost killed themselves with the effort they put in," Armand said.

"We will return to Cape Town tomorrow then decide what we will do next, once we are replenished."

# Chapter 14: Finishing Up

It took them over three weeks to make the return trip as the prevailing wind was all wrong, but they eventually got there. Marty took the time to write a detailed report for Wickham and added a chapter or two to his letters to Caroline, his mother, the de Marchets, and Miss Kate.

When they tied up at the dock, they saw a British Frigate anchored in the bay with half a dozen East Indiamen. They looked to have had a hard voyage and were making repairs.

The Lark and Alouette were both carrying the scars of their battles and the crews walked proudly, if a little unsteadily on the docks.

A boat came across from the Frigate, which turned out to be the Seahorse under Captain Stewart, who had escorted the convoy down from England.

The midshipman brought mail and an invitation for them to dine aboard.

The mail was distributed, and Marty saw he had private letters from Caroline, Miss Kate, and the de Marchets along with ones from his bank and prize agent. There were also official packets from the Admiralty, Wickham, and the palace.

He opened the one from the palace first. It was an official confirmation of his barony and a letter informing him that he was being enrolled in the Order Of The Bath. He didn't know what that was, but it sounded kind of odd.

The letter from the Admiralty was just the usual updates of signals and requests for the lists.

The one from Wickham was more interesting and in code. Once he had decoded it, he read that:

Their explosive endeavours in Paris hadn't caused the Coup d'état by Napoleon as they had now received new information that it had been in planning for a long time. Napoleon was indeed suing for peace and the government was desperate to agree to one as the war was bankrupting the country. However, they had gone a long way to securing the future of the S.O.F. and any good news that they could bring back would help as well. He told that he had discretely discussed their mission with the senior members of the Honourable East India Company and if they were to be successful, then a significant reward would be forthcoming. Unofficially, of course. He was to look out for two of those honourable gentlemen who were heading to India.

Marty wondered what that meant. Had Wickham used this mission to enlist the support of the company in keeping the S.O.F. going? If he had what did that mean for the future?

The letters from the de Marchets were filled with news and details of the preparations for Evelyn's wedding. There were also copies of newspapers with the announcements. Marty put them aside to enjoy later.

The letter from Miss Katy was full of news about his family and how his marriage to Caroline and his barony had made them local celebrities. His mother was being pestered by suitors who suddenly found her to be a 'good catch,' but he need not worry as his brothers were fronting up and protecting her from unwanted attention. That had resulted in a few bruises and even a broken arm so far. She passed on a message from his brother, Arthur, who said that he was doing well in the forge and had a commission to create a pair of large wrought iron gates for a big country house. He had to take on a couple of helpers to make them, but he hoped that it would lead to further work of the type.

Last, he read the letters from Caroline. They told of how much she missed him but understood he had his duty. The pregnancy was progressing normally and just after he left, she started getting morning sickness. *That doesn't sound nice,* he thought. The distribution of brandy and wine 'imported' by the Deal boys was going well and she had come to an agreement with Bill Clarence that she would be their exclusive distributor. Marty wondered at the legality of the whole activity, but it was her hobby, so he let it pass. She also said that Bill was helping her with the distribution business and was now more a business partner than a supplier.

If he didn't know that Bill was madly in love with his wife, Stella, he would have been jealous.

He suddenly realised that the baby was due in July, and there was no chance that they would get home in time for the birth. That upset him quite a bit, and he immediately added a paragraph to break the news to his letter to her.

He sealed his letters and put them in the mail bag that would be left with the Port Admiral to be put on the next ship home.

That evening, he met Armand on the Alouette and asked him whether he had received a letter from Wickham. He hadn't, so he filled him in on what it had said. Armand didn't appear to be bothered that Wickham had written to Marty and not him.

They boated across to the Seahorse and were greeted by a full side party at the entry. They were escorted down into the captain's dining room and found themselves in the company of not just the captain but two men who were introduced as commissioners for the Honourable East India Company. Sir Rodney Chapman and the honourable Stanley Winchcombe esquire.

Winchcombe started to call Marty M'Lord, but he was quickly corrected by Marty, who insisted that he only use his Navy rank. Captain Stewart looked relieved as he had no idea how to cope with someone the rank of a baron who was also a lieutenant.

They sat down in comfortable chairs over glasses of Madera, and, after some small talk, Sir Rodney asked if their mission had produced any results. Marty looked at Captain Stewart and saw he looked interested.

"I have had a letter from England," he opened, "Are you the gentlemen referred to?"

"Yes, we have spoken to your – aah – sponsor. He advised us to talk to you directly. The good Captain is sworn to secrecy," Sir Rodney smiled.

Marty exchanged a glance with Armand. Curiouser and curiouser, *what the hell is going on?* He thought.

"Under the guise of French privateers, we made contact with a nest of pirates on the mainland just where the straits between there and Madagascar are the narrowest. We were fortunate to meet with two Moroccan gentlemen who purported to be envoys for the Sultan of Morocco."

"Did they, bedamned!" exclaimed Winchcombe.

Marty ignored the interruption and continued,

"We implanted the idea that we were privateers, licensed by the French government to 'work' the straits and take East Indiamen to disrupt British trade. They then let slip that they had an exclusive agreement with the revolutionary government that they had those rights. So, we told them that there had been a change of government and they were out of business."

"Oh, that's rich!" Laughed Sir Rodney. "And what was their reaction?"

"Well, Armand was in Port Antisiranana at the same time. Spreading the word that the revolution was over and that there was new management in place. A dhow arrived, we think from the emissaries, and all hell broke loose. He left town quickly and we rendezvoused to the south." Marty paused to take a sip of drink.

"That was it?" Asked Captain Stewart.

"No." Armand said taking up the story. "We thought to set a trap for the pirates on the mainland and deliberately sailed past their base. What we didn't expect was a reinforced fleet of ships waiting for us."

He then went on to describe the action.

"Good god!" Sir Rodney exclaimed at the end of the tale. "You may have destroyed their capability to attack our ships completely."

Marty looked up at that and said,

"That we cannot claim, not until we go and have another look around the island."

Captain Stewart intervened at that point and said,

"I am sure you have further plans but didn't I read that Lady Caroline was with child?"

*Nice change of subject,* Marty thought and replied,

"Yes, she is, but I doubt I will return home in time for the birth."

There were mutters of sympathy at that then the steward called them to dinner.

Over dinner, Stewart asked them about the armament of their ships and, when told, spluttered.

"Damn unconventional!"

"But effective," Marty smiled.

"Can you elucidate us poor landlubbers on that?" asked Winchcombe.

"We carry mainly carronades and only four long nines between us," Marty explained, "They are much more effective at close range a bit like huge blunderbuss. But ours throw twelve, four-pound balls or twenty-four pounds of grape. We can also throw a single twenty-four-pound ball which will demolish just about anything."

"But you have to get within, what, three cables to be accurate," stated Captain Stewart.

"That's no problem," quipped Marty, "we just let them come and then surprise the hell out of them."

The dinner ended soon after that, and the two lieutenants made their unsteady way back to their boat.

They restocked with powder and shot the next afternoon. They had already filled up the water kegs and taken on as much fresh meat, veg, and fruit as they could. As the tide turned, they slipped out of the harbour and set course for Madagascar. It took them ten days and this time, they steered around the east coast of the island. They checked every bay and inlet for boats. If they found any, they burned them unless they were clearly just fishing boats.

They came up to a large bay that ran some fifty miles to the Northwest and was twenty plus miles wide. Inside it towards the end was a fleet of some fifteen Dhows. Some were armed and others not, but it made no difference to Marty and Armand they descended on them like avenging angels. Carronades spitting fire and belching smoke, dealing out pain and death to anyone who stood against them.

Once they were done, they turned back to the North and sailed up the coast to the Northern most tip of the Island. Antisiranana lay at their feet.

As they approached, fishing boats turned and fled back into the harbour. Terrified fishermen had heard of the devils without mercy.

Marty looked across the sea towards the entrance and saw a large, triangular, grey fin come towards them and circle the Lark once. Marty could see the huge but graceful shape under the water. The giant shark had found them again. It settled down parallel to them staying about sixty feet off their starboard side. "Don't worry mate, you will get your lunch soon enough," Marty thought.

The lookout hailed the deck and called,

"A COUPLE OF XEBECS MAKING SAIL IN THE HARBOUR." A pause, then, "ANOTHER APPROACHING FROM THE NORTH."

*Another trap,* Marty grinned to himself. He and Armand had discussed this, and they had come up with a couple of different plans.

James spoke.

"Signal from the Alouette. The number eight over the number two."

Marty now knew exactly what Armand would do.

"Make all sail," he commanded and after James had shouted the orders.

"Load smashers in all guns." This was what they called the big twenty-four-pound balls. Their strategy depended on their agility and speed to out sail the enemy ships. Then hit them where it hurt.

James came and stood beside him. Blaez appeared from where he had been snoozing and sat on his left. Tom and John came up from below and John took the helm. Tom took his place behind Marty. He looked down the deck and there were his three remaining Basques. He nodded, and they moved to stand one on either beam with Matai at the bow.

It was quiet, only the faint creak of the rigging and sloosh of the water running down the hull could be heard. They turned to go head-to-head with the Northern Xebec.

The Alouette made for the harbour entrance all sail set. She would try and blockade the other two Xebecs at the entrance, if she could, and deal them some pain from her smashers and long nines.

Marty focused. They had the weather gage and could dictate what happened next. As they got closer, he could see that there were men lining the rail shaking their fists and weapons at them. "My oh my, they are pissed off," he smiled to himself, "Good, angry men make mistakes."

"James, I will sail up their larboard side at about four cables distance. If their shooting is as bad as Armand said, we should be safe enough. As soon as we are level with their stern, I want the mainsail taken in fast and we will swing around behind him. We will serve him alternately from either battery. Do you understand?"

James absorbed what he said and nodded.

"Try and get their rudder if you can, I want her disabled."

'Aye aye, sir," he said with a smile

"Tom, please command the starboard battery. Make sure of your shots."

Tom said nothing, just moved down to take position behind his five carronades.

They were closing fast. Marty settled his weapons harness then knelt down and gave Blaez a hug.

When he stood, they were almost bow to bow with the Xebec and he raised his arm.

Matai threw back his head and gave out the cry,

"Eye, Yiy, Yiy, Yiy, Yiy, Yiy, Yiy, Yiy, Yiy Yeeehhhaaa!"

It was answered by Antton.

"Eye, Yiy, Yiy, Yiy, Yiy, Yiy, Yiy, Yiy, Yiy Yeeehhhaaa, Yiy!"

Then Garai.

"Eye, Yiy, Yiy, Yiy, Yiy, Yiy, Yiy, Yiy, Yiy Yeeehhhaaa! Eye, Yiy."

And then the whole crew. As it died away, Marty could see shocked looks on the faces of the men lining the Xebecs side and he yelled,

"FIRE!"

The five larboard carronades belched flame and smoke and simultaneously he saw a ripple of fire from the Xebecs side. Their shot mostly fell behind them with only one ball even getting close. His shot had more effect. His men were schooled at firing at fast crossing targets and knew what they were about. At least three hits were scored, and the smashers lived up to their names. Big holes appeared in her side and they could see splinters flying everywhere.

Then the mainsail dropped, and Marty signalled John Smith to steer hard to Larboard. The gun crews were reloading in a controlled frenzy. They swung around in an arc and were soon dead astern of the Xebec. She had tried to match they turn but with their agility they easily beat her to it. Now, they had to stop her before she could get to the Alouette.

He brought them up rapidly to about a cable behind her. It all depended now on the Xebec trying to get to the Alouette and not trying to turn and fight the little wasp behind them.

He shouted, "JAMES!" and signaled John to swing the bow to starboard. As the guns came to bear, they fired in succession. As soon as the last fired, he ordered a swing back to larboard and Tom fired his off.

The effect on the vulnerable stern of the Xebec was devastating. The transom was completely smashed in leaving a gaping hole. But by some miracle the rudder was still working!

The guns were re-loaded, and he did the same manoeuvres again, this time the boys aimed lower and after the third gun fired, he saw the Xebec fall off the wind, out of control. Her rudder was gone.

He called orders to heave to a cable off her larboard quarter and proceeded to pound her to matchwood.

He got the lookout to check what was happening back at the harbour and heard that one of the Xebecs was on fire and the other was being engaged by the Alouette. Armand had done his job as well.

Suddenly, the lookout called,

"SAIL HO, WEST NORWEST." A pause.

"LOOKS LIKE A BLOODY NAVY FRIGATE!"

Marty grabbed a telescope and ran up the ratlines to where the lookout was perched and took a long, hard look himself.

"That's the Seahorse!" he said to the lookout. He slid down a stay to the deck and called for his men to cease fire. The Xebec was a wreck and wouldn't swim for much longer. He walked across to the rail and watched it for a while. He was about to step away when something grabbed him by the shoulder and spun him around, sending him crashing to the deck.

The world spun, and he heard James screaming for the men to open fire and then Tom was there and holding him in his arms. The pain came and the world went black.

# Chapter 15: Homeward Bound.

He woke briefly to intense pain and was conscious of someone holding him down and being unable to move his arms. He could hear Blaez barking insanely then it all went black again.

He came to in his cabin with the sun shining in the transom windows. As he gathered his awareness, he realised the ship was stationary. His eyes were gummy, and he had to blink a few times to be able to see anything clearly.

A face appeared. It took a moment to recognise it as belonging to the surgeon from the Alouette.

"Hello. Back with us I see," he said unnecessarily.

"Mwuf," Marty said.

A moist cloth was placed against his lips and some moisture trickled into his mouth. He tried again.

"What happened?" he mumbled.

"You were shot. Got you in the right shoulder. Actually, was a damn fine shot from over one hundred yards."

Marty had a moment of absolute terror and tried to see if his arm was still there. He couldn't see, and he tried to sit.

The surgeon (still couldn't remember his name) pushed him gently back on the bed and said,

"Its alright! You still have your arm and in time will get the full use of it again. But now, you must rest. You lost a lot of blood and that damn dog of yours bit five men trying to get to you. Caused more damage than the bloody pirates."

Marty started to laugh at the picture that painted but stopped when it sent shooting pains down his arm and across his back.

Later that day, James and Tom came in to see him and he asked to see Blaez. It turned out that Matai was the only one who could get near him and brought him in on his leash. The frantic dog scrabbled and fought his way across the floor and would have jumped on the bed if Marty hadn't given a clear command to sit.

As it was, the sound of Marty's voice calmed him and he sat beside the bed so he could rest his head on the cover and look at Marty with worried eyes.

"Hello boy," Marty said, "It's ok, you can stay here now."

Blaez gave a huff and a look that said, 'I'm not going anywhere, boss'.

They were in Cape Town harbour, and he got visits from the Admiral and local dignitaries. They got mail from home, but the letters were old and all he knew was, that Caroline was fine and the baby was due soon. Then just as he was getting back to his feet after a couple of weeks, the Seahorse came back into harbour.

Captain Stewart and the two East India Company commissars came over in a boat, and he met them with Armand in his cabin.

"Lieutenant Stockley, we hope you are making a full recovery?" said Sir Rodney.

"Yes, thank you," Marty replied, "My arm will be stiff for a while, but the surgeon assures me that with the right exercise I will be as right as rain."

"Excellent, Excellent," murmured all three men.

Captain Stewart coughed and said,

"To all intents and purposes, you two gentlemen and your band of cutthroats have ripped the heart out of the pirate activity based around Madagascar and the East African coast. I doubt they could put together four boats with what you have left them." He looked from one to the other.

"Your tactics and strategies are most certainly not in the Navy book of warfare but were most effective all the same. I can see why Lord Hood formed you into a special unit."

Marty must have looked worried at that.

Stewart smiled reassuringly.

"Don't worry, we are all sworn to secrecy by both Hood and Wickham."

Sir Rodney was looking impatient, and Armand looked to him and raised his eyebrows in question. He coughed and then sat upright like he was about to make an announcement.

"Gentlemen. The Board of the East India Company and its shareholders are in your debt. We understand the sacrifice and dedication you have shown to this enterprise will not result in any prize money, fame, or promotion. You and your crews embarked on this purely out of duty."

Marty's shoulder was throbbing, and he was thinking, *where the hell is this leading.* But Sir Rodney was in full flow.

"Accordingly, we are going to recommend that each and every crewman is awarded a sum of one hundred pounds and that that the estates of those that fell will receive the sum in their stead."

Marty was surprised, and he thanked them for their extreme generosity on behalf of the men.

Winchcombe then lent forward and said,

"Now, we come to you two gentlemen. We realise that you are both independently wealthy, so a cash reward would be meaningless."

"So, we are going to offer you something more meaningful. We will open the door to you becoming shareholders of the company. In public, this will be just like any other transaction, but you will be able to buy shares at half price up to a predefined limit. Once vested, you will be invited to invest in high value shipments and place supercargo on any company ship."

Phew! That was some reward!

"Lastly," Captain Stewart put in, "We will escort you back to England. The Seahorse is returning for a refit, so it makes sense to stay together. Would you want to stay on the Lark or be my guest onboard the Seahorse while you recover from your wound, Mr. Stockley?"

"Thank you for the kind offer," Marty replied, "But I will stay with my ship. My men deserve that."

"I completely understand," Stewart replied before the other two could object.

They got underway the next day and the three ships made their way out of the harbour on the morning tide. Seahorse in the lead, then Alouette and finally the Lark in line astern a cable apart. The weather was fine, and Marty was thankful that there were only lazy rollers crossing the Atlantic. He wasn't sure he could handle a big sea just yet.

The journey back took them out to roughly mid Atlantic to pick up the trades and then turned Northeast at around twenty-three degrees North. It took two and a half months and they stopped at Ascension Island to replenish.

They left the Seahorse as it entered Plymouth. The frigate's crew lined the sides and the yards and gave them a huge cheer in farewell. They carried on to their home base. Marty sent a message to Caroline via Captain Stewart that they would be docking in the next few days.

It was mid-September when they sailed up the Stour and turned to dock. Marty could see several people waiting for them and used a small telescope to look for Caroline. He couldn't see her at first but then he recognised her coach and saw her stepping out of it with a bundle in her arms.

As soon as the boat docked, Marty jumped over the side and ran to his love. He took her gently in his arms and kissed her. Then he leaned back to look down at the now three-month-old child in her arms.

"Martin, meet Bethany Anne Stockley. Your daughter," she said with tears in her eyes.

Marty was transfixed as he looked at the beautiful baby girl. Caroline held her out for him to take her and then realised something.

"Anne? After my mother?"

"Yes, she came and lived with me for the last three months and insisted on helping with the delivery."

"She would. She's been present at all of her grandchildren's births." Marty laughed.

He turned and walked back down the dock and stood between the two ships. He held his daughter high in the air and shouted,

"This is my daughter! Bethany Anne. Say welcome, you pirates!"

Both crews roared their greeting and then all of the Larks gave their war cry,

"Eye, Yiy, Yiy, Yiy, Yiy, Yiy, Yiy, Yiy, Yiy Yeeehhhaaa!"

Caroline looked startled, and Marty laughed but had a tear in his eye as he remembered Paolo.

Little Bethany, Beth in his mind, didn't bat an eyelid just waved her chubby arms.

Back at the farm, he had to tell Caroline about his wound and she wasn't happy. She insisted he take off his shirt and show it to her. She then roasted his ears for a good five minutes for being careless and then burst into tears and hugged him.

Women, he thought, I'll never understand them.

After a debriefing with Wickham and Lord Hood, who showed up the next morning, everyone was given shore leave for the next two or three months. The ships would be sailed to Chatham, by skeleton crews led by the mids, for a refit. Once in the hands of the Navy yard, the crews could go home as well.

Marty knew the Basques had no one to go to and neither did Tom so he told Caroline that they would be coming with him. He was surprised when Tom asked if Wilson could tag along as well as he came from Manchester and that was up near there as well.

Caroline said they would go to Cheshire via London and Marty was happy to just let her take the reins.

In London, he had to assume his alter ego as Lord Candor. It didn't sit easily. They had a stream of visitors in the few days they were there and a host of invites to parties and balls. Marty also discovered that they had a nanny for the baby. Caroline fed it and cuddled it, but the nanny looked after it for most of the day.

This was new for Marty, and he wasn't sure how he felt about it. He had been brought up in his family by his mother. Well, his mother and his sisters, he realised. They would spell his mother and look after him when she wasn't able or was ill. After some thought, he concluded, this wasn't that different.

They left London and headed to the family estate in Cheshire. This was Marty's first visit, and he didn't know what to expect. It was near somewhere called Knutsford, but he didn't have a clear idea where that was either.

There were two coaches and a wagon as Caroline had been shopping and they needed the wagon for her purchases. The boys rode in the second and took it in turns to ride guard on Marty and Caroline's. Blaez either rode inside with him and Caroline or ran alongside.

No highwayman would stand a chance if he tried to rob them, and Marty sincerely hoped one wouldn't try. Not because he was afraid, but it would be inconvenient having to explain away a body with probably a dozen balls in it.

It took several days to get to Knutsford, which was pleasant little village. As they passed through the locals waved to the coach and Caroline waved back.

Just outside they turned off the road through a pair of grand wrought iron gates and up a well-maintained driveway. The drive was lined with chestnut and beech trees. Was around a mile long and wove through parkland with wild deer and horses in paddocks surrounded by wood rail fences.

A large grand country house soon came into view. Marty's chin almost hit his chest. It was enormous! It was mix of styles as it looked to have evolved over time and been added to by each generation. It was, in fact, the administrative heart of the estate which covered more than three thousand acres, had hundreds of tenants and whole villages within its boundaries.

The coach pulled up at the entrance where a whole line of people stood outside. Some in uniform, others in normal clothes. The coachman pulled up and a young man in uniform placed some steps at the coach door and opened it with a bow.

Caroline stepped down first and waited for Marty at the steps. Blaez followed him out and stuck like glue to his left knee, unsure what was going on. Marty led him to the other coach and gave him to Matai to look after.

Caroline took him by the hand when he returned to her side and led him to the centre of the line.

"Martin," she said to him, "May I introduce you to our household staff?"

He nodded, not sure what to say.

She took him to the end of the line where the most senior and grandly dressed were stood. An imposing man in a black suit, white shirt and tie was first in line.

"Martin, this is George, our Butler," Marty held out his hand and the man looked surprised but took it and said,

"A pleasure to meet you, M'Lord."

They moved to the next in line and Caroline whispered, "You don't have to shake all their hands."

He moved down the line and met the housekeeper, the cook, the Senior Maid downstairs, the head footman, the gamekeeper and so on down the entire line until the Maid of all works, a young girl of about fourteen. He stepped back and saw the grinning faces of his men standing around their coach.

Caroline nudged him and said,

"You need to say a few words to them."

It took Marty a second to realise she meant the staff.

He walked back to the centre of the line.

"Thank you for your kind welcome," he started, "As you know, my experience is in running a ship not a house. So, you will not find me interfering or changing the way things are run. I will be here in between my duties as a king's officer and will often be accompanied by some of my crew." He looked over to the men. "So, there are no misunderstandings, let me introduce you to them."

He beckoned them over and put his hand on Tom's shoulder.

"This is Tom Savage, and he is my cox. That is my right-hand man onboard ship." He pointed to Wilson.

"That giant is Wilson; the three swarthy gentlemen are from the land of the Basques. They are, what we call in the Navy, my followers and accompany me everywhere I go." *Well almost,* he thought. "They will be staying here with me while we are on shore leave."

He sort of ran out of words after that, thanked them all again, and let Caroline show him inside.

He went upstairs to change and found an old man in his room.

"Good afternoon, sir," he quavered, "I am Simon, your valet. I have hung your clothes and put away most of your things, but I didn't know what to do with these." He indicated a table where he had laid out the weapons Marty had put in his chest.

*Looks a lot when they're laid out like that,* Marty thought.

"Is there a spare cupboard?" asked Marty, looking around the room.

"The bottom drawer of the sideboard is empty, Sir," Simon replied.

Marty went over and opened it.

"That should be big enough," he said and started transferring first his knives and then his pistols into it.

"In the bedroom, sir?"

Marty looked over his shoulder and smiled.

"They wouldn't be much good down in the cellar would they."

He removed the two barkers he had in his coat pockets, blew out the priming into the fireplace and put them in as well.

He started to take off his jacket when Simon stepped up to help him. He caught the look on Simon's face in a mirror when he saw the knife on the back of his belt. The old man's eyes went round, and his mouth made an Oh! Marty had to hide a smile when he unbuttoned his cuffs and undid the wrist sheaths with their stilettoes in and took a throwing knife out of the hidden sheath in his right boot.

"Never in all my years!" He exclaimed. "I was the old Lord's valet for thirty years and never saw such a thing!"

"Standard dress," Marty quipped, "Now, I would like a bath then get dressed for dinner."

"Will sir be needing these?" Simon asked, waving a hand at the drawer.

"No, just this one," Marty said and slid the sheath off his belt.

To give the old man due credit, he took that square on the chin without a flinch.

"There were two wrapped packages in my chest where did you put those?"

"Over there on the dressing table, sir."

"Presents for my wife." He grinned. "It's her birthday tomorrow".

"I know, sir. She is very dear to all of us."

Marty looked at the old man, saw the sincerity in his eyes and just nodded. He hid the packages in the bottom drawer with his armoury.

He went downstairs early for dinner and passed Caroline on the stairs. She looked him up and down and smiled.

"You met Simon then."

"Yes. Nice old chap."

"You changing?" He asked, stopping and turning to watch her glide up the stairs.

"Of course," she replied over her shoulder.

"No time for . . .?"

"No. Dinner is at seven." She grinned over shoulder. Just as she entered their bedroom, she turned and said, "But we could have an early night!"

The next morning over breakfast, all the staff came in and sang happy birthday to her. It had only taken a suggestion to George the butler, and he had organised it with a certain amount of glee. *He wasn't as stiff as he appeared,* Marty thought.

Marty handed her the packages, and she opened the first one to gasps from the staff. In it, were a pair of matched muff pistols. These were small, single barrelled guns that a lady could hide in her fur muff (a hand warmer normally slung on a string at waist height). These were exquisitely made and chased in silver.

"Oh Martin, they are beautiful," she cried then with a frown, "Are they loaded?"

"No, I thought it best not to at breakfast." He laughed

She put them aside and picked up the second present which was wrapped in silk and tied with a bow.

She opened it and sighed. Inside was a golden locket on a beautiful chain. The locket was oval and over an inch from top to bottom. It was engraved with their initials intertwined.

She pressed the catch to open it and inside were two beautifully painted miniatures of them both. She gazed at it with tears in her eyes and stood to go to him. He stood as well, and they met around mid-table and exchanged a passionate kiss.

There was a discrete cough from behind him, and Marty realised all the servants were still there. The younger girls blushing pink and the boys sniggering.

He laughed, took the chain in his hands, and fastened it around Caroline's neck. The staff applauded politely.

The door to the dining room swung open and Tom led the boys in. They were carrying a large picture frame covered in a sheet.

Marty looked surprised and Caroline intrigued. They set in on a chair at the end of the room so the light from the morning sun shone on it.

"The men o' the Lark wanted you to have something from them all for your birthday, Lady Caroline," Tom announced, "So, they talked to a mate of our'n who be a fair hand and he done this fer us."

He pulled the sheet aside revealing a painting of the Snipe under full sail on a stormy sea. Marty was amazed as the likeness was perfect and the brushwork fine.

"It looks like a Charles Brooking!" Caroline decided. "But he died in '59."

"Well, our mate is a dab hand at copyin' so he might have 'borrowed' a bit from that Brooking feller," Tom admitted.

"A forger?" Marty asked.

"Well, I wouldn't go that far," Tom said looking a bit uncomfortable.

"It can't be a forgery it's an original," Caroline declared.

Tom looked at Marty triumphantly.


A week later, Marty and Tom were out walking with Blaez. They were both carrying shotguns in case they saw a bird or rabbit for the pot. Marty also had a sling looped through his belt.

"I was thinking of doing a tour of the estate and meeting the tenant and estate workers," Marty told him.

"Sounds like the right thing to do. Men always like to meet the man in charge," Tom replied.

"You can ride with me."

"You want me to get some o' the boys to come too?"

Marty thought about that.

"No. I don't think so. I want to meet the tenants not intimidate them."

A pheasant flew up from right under Blaez's nose and he jumped straight up in the air in surprise. Marty's gun was up and fired in one smooth motion.

He walked over and picked it up. Blaez was many things but not a retriever. They got home with three brace of birds and handed them over to the cook.

Marty told Caroline of his plan in bed that night and she whole heartedly approved. So, the next morning, he and Tom set off with the Estate Manager acting as guide.

Marty noted which houses were kept in good repair and which were looking dilapidated. He asked questions of every tenant and worker he met and made notes in a small notebook he carried in his pocket.

After three days, he sat with Caroline and the Estate Manager, Farrell Mountjoy.

"Our people fall into three categories," he explained.

"Those that look after their properties and land. Those that aren't able to look after either because they are too old or impaired. And last those that don't look after either because they are lazy and just look to the estate to provide food."

Mountjoy agreed.

"We have a duty to care for the old and infirm as they have given their lives to the estate and deserve it. But those who are fit to work and don't choose to take care of the place they live in or provide something for themselves, we don't."

"What do you suggest we do?" Caroline asked.

"Carrot and stick. We reward those that do, and we punish those that don't."

They looked at him expectantly.

"Alright, I will explain. We will send out work crews and bring every building on the estate up to standard.

Every property that needs no work will be rewarded with a cash gift.

If the person is old or infirm and unable to work, we do the work for free.

If they are fit, we deduct the costs from their pay over the next year, up to a maximum of a third. We also start deducting pay for food supplied outside of what we give as part of their package."

"How many are in the third group?" Caroline asked.

Marty checked his figures.

"About a tenth. That's, let me see, twelve households."

"Oh, and in that group, I also saw several wives with bruises that looked like they were beaten and kids that were underfed. I would place money on the men drinking all the money."

"Sounds like a spell in the Navy would sort them out," Caroline muttered.

"What?" said Marty.

"I said a spell in the Navy would fix them."

Martin looked thoughtful.

"Do we know what work these men do?" Marty asked Mountjoy.

He referred to a ledger and said,

"Yes, they are nearly all labourers, one is a dry wall builder, another a ditch digger." He continued looking them up one by one.

"So, no one who couldn't be easily replaced?"

"No. All easy jobs to fill."

"Could the women be given work if the men were removed?"

"I have had an idea to start a dairy to make cheese. We have a lot more milk than we use, and we just send it off the estate and get practically nothing for it. Cheese sells for a much better price. A dozen women would make that possible," said Caroline, "But what about the children? Who looks after them if the women are working?"

"We could set up a school for the kids while the mothers are working," added Marty, thinking of Katy Turner.

At the end of the month, work crews started renovating all the properties on the estate and building a new dairy parlour and a schoolhouse. When that was finished, a press gang mysteriously appeared, picked up twelve men and a couple of older boys and took them off to Liverpool where they 'joined' the Navy. Their wives were offered jobs in the new dairy in return for keeping their houses and a living wage. Their children would also receive a primary education. All but one of the women took them up on the offer. She went to live with her parents in Manchester.

Marty started looking into the latest theories in land management and was just really getting into it when...

A packet arrived sealed with the fouled anchor accompanied by a courier. Marty sent the courier to the kitchens and settled into his study to read the letter inside. There was a knock at the door. Tom came in, leaned on the mantle, and waited.

Marty read the orders once and reread the important bits again.

"It's from Lord Hood in his own hand. The Admiralty has a problem they can't fix in the normal way. He wants us to fix that problem in any way we see fit."

He got up and checked the corridor outside of the door then closed it. He beckoned Tom to stand by him as far from the door as they could.

"There is a Captain of a Frigate who is in the position because he is a personal friend of the Prince Regent and strongly supported by the prince's political cronies. Apparently, he is as mad as a bat and nasty with it. They can't remove him without starting an internal war that they don't want, but they need the ship in reliable hands. The crew are close to mutiny as well. They don't want that either as it could spread."

"Hmph, just the job for us then," Tom quipped sarcastically.

"We need John with us. Can you message him to meet us in Portsmouth in ten days?"

"Aye, I will."

Marty went and found Caroline who was in the new dairy and broke the news. She had seen the courier arrive so was expecting it. She hugged him and sent him off to pack.

Simon appeared and helped him with his sea chest. After all the uniforms were in, folded with tissue paper, he went to the bottom door of the cabinet and asked.

"Do you want to take all of them or just a selection?"

Marty thought for a second or two and said,

"The double-barrelled pistols, the stilettoes, and the boot knife. The rest can stay." He smiled as the old man carefully took each knife and wrapped it in a piece of oiled cloth. Then he made sure the ball moulds, powder flask, wads and spare flints were in the pistols box along with cleaning tools and oil.

"Have you been in the Army or Navy, Simon?"

"I was his Lordship's batman in the days he was in the cavalry."

"So, that's how you know how to treat blades then."

"Yes sir. His Lordship was very particular about that. Will you be gone long sir?"

"I don't know, but at least three months, I think. Why?"

"Well, her Ladyship misses you awfully when you are gone and worries something terrible about you."

"And my letters don't arrive every week," Marty finished for him.

"Yes sir."

"We don't always see a homeward bound ship or go into a friendly port where we can leave our mail. The best we can do is write something every day and send it when we can."

"So, you don't get her letters either?"

"Not often and they tend to all arrive at once when they do."

"The Navy is a hard life then, for married men."

"Yes, they prefer their younger officers to be single, but they made an exception for me." Marty smiled.

# Chapter 16: Into Insanity

They left at first light the next morning. Blaez had to stay behind, which he wasn't happy about, but he had made very good friends with a pretty border collie bitch. So, he didn't mind that much. It would take several days to get to Portsmouth even by one of his own coaches.

Their cover story was; the boys had been ordered to join the ship to replace crew that had 'had accidents', Marty to replace the second lieutenant who had just walked away when they came into dock.

They arrived in Portsmouth to find John Smith waiting for them. They soon identified the Sunderland in the harbour. She was the one that looked like a 'whore's boudoir" as John succinctly put it. She was tidy, in fact, over tidy to the point of looking unused. All the yards crossed just so and not a rope out of place, as far as they could see. The paintwork was too perfect, looking like it had never seen weather. The gingerbread work around the stern gleamed with gold leaf. Sunlight glinted off polished metalwork.

Strangely, they could see no movement. There didn't appear to be anybody on watch and there was no indication that she was out of discipline. No boats approached her either.

Marty hailed a boatman and asked him to ferry them out. The man looked reluctant and only agreed after Marty paid a pair of crowns, which was about double the going rate.

They approached the ship and were almost hooking on before a voice hailed, "Boat ahoy." The boatman signalled he had an officer onboard.

"Who are you?" Called the voice.

"Lieutenant Martin Stockley and six men here to join the ship," Marty barked in an impatient tone. This was most irregular.

"Wait there," the voice commanded.

They waited for several minutes then there was a clatter of footsteps and barked orders. Side boys appeared and held out the pristinely clean side ropes then a sour looking face in a lieutenant's uniform looked down and said,

"Well don't just sit there. Get aboard!"

Marty looked at Tom and raised his eyebrows but got himself onto the battens and climbed the side. As his head cleared the deck, he could see a row of smartly dressed Marines with an officer in charge, several ships officers, and a man dressed in something that vaguely impersonated a Navy uniform but was so fancy it would have been at home on the Prince Regent. He also had makeup on his face. Rouged cheeks, and a beauty spot.

He reached the deck, saluted the quarterdeck, and said,

"Lieutenant Stockley reporting aboard as Second Lieutenant."

The overdressed fop stepped forward, made a florid overdone bow and said.

"My Lord Candor! Welcome! Welcome! We are graced by your presence!"

*Oh My God, he's as mad as bucket of frogs,* thought Marty, *well if he wants to play that game, let's dance.*

"Captain Carruthers. My pleasure, sir," Marty replied in his best smarmy voice and bowed back to the correct angle protocol demanded.

"I have orders to join you and have six replacements, followers of mine," he added looking at what he assumed was the first lieutenant.

The Captain looked to the man who had ordered them up and said,

"Jonny, be a good chap and get those men up and made comfortable."

'Jonny' Gave Marty a dirty look and started giving orders in a quiet voice.

"Come, come!" The Captain insisted, taking Marty by the arm, and leading him astern.

They approached his cabin. The marine on guard, wasn't in marine uniform but a footman's outfit, opened the door for them and bowed them in.

Marty almost stopped at the door as he got his first view of the inside. It looked like the living room of a palace! Tapestries covered the walls and the transom windows had chintz curtains. The chairs were lush and overstuffed and there was no desk. There were even fresh cut flowers on the sideboard.

The Captain flopped down in one of the chairs and indicated he should sit in the other. Marty lowered himself in noting how soft the chairs were. He waited.

"I am so pleased you have joined us aboard our ship," the Captain simpered. "When we found out it was you who they were sending we could hardly contain ourselves."

*What is with all the 'we's' and 'us's,* Marty thought.

"Our royal person gets so tired of dealing with the uncultured oafs under our command," he sighed.

*Damn me, he things he's the bloody king!* Marty realised. He was on dangerous ground. He was smart enough to know that if he popped the man's fantasy or even contradicted him, he could be punished or worse, killed. So, he decided to play along and see where it took him.

"I absolutely understand. Your…?"

"Oh, highness will do," the Captain chirped brightly.

*Nope, he thinks he is the prince regent.*

"Your highness," Marty completed.

"Having to travel down with untitled, uneducated dolts, even if they are my followers, is very trying."

"I wanted to make you first, you know," the Captain said conspiratorially. "But Jonny got so angry I didn't have the heart to demote him. After all he practically runs this ship, you know."

"Good staff are so hard to find," Marty agreed.

"Now, I must not keep you from settling in. We must meet every day and have a chat and a glass of wine." He looked thoughtful for a moment and then said,

"Would you give me the pleasure of your company this evening for dinner? Drinks at a half past seven?"

"Delighted, delighted, your highness," Marty said as he stood to leave.

As Marty stepped out on deck, the first lieutenant was on watch on the quarterdeck.

"Mr. Stockley, report to me now," he ordered.

Marty climbed the steps and presented himself. He didn't get a chance to say anything.

"If you think you will be replacing me as first, you will find you will have bitten off more than you can chew," the man snarled and when Marty made to respond, cut him off and moved very close so no one else could hear. "I will see you broken, and all your followers flogged to death before I am finished if you so much as put a single toe out of line. This is my ship and that fool below is just a passenger. You keep him happy, and your men are safe."

He stepped back, and Marty could see the pupils of his eyes were very dilated. Then he seemed to shake himself and said,

"We sail on the tide. Make sure the ship is ready and get those slobs up and on watch."

"Aye Aye, sir," Marty said, and went to rouse the mates.

They got to sea. The crew were well drilled but worked in absolute silence and cast frightened glances aft to the quarterdeck. Marty had no chance to talk to any of his men to find out how it was below decks, but he suspected that it was ruled by the lash. The Captain told him they had been ordered to sail North to the Shetlands to put on a show of support to the natives.

Marty suspected the orders were just contrived to get the ship out of harbour so he could get to work.

Marty had been below to check the stores and, on his way back to the wardroom, ran into the purser. A weaselly little man with a squint that sent his eyes off in different directions.

"Mr. Sales," he greeted him, "Have the men been issued with cold weather clothes for the North Atlantic?"

"Extra clothes? What will they need them for?"

Marty looked at him closely to see if he was being funny and realized he genuinely didn't know.

"Have you ever been to the North Atlantic in winter?"

'No, never been there."

"It is cold enough to have ice form on the spars and rigging. The men will need warmer clothes than what they have now to be able to function."

"Well, I won't issue any, unless ordered by the Captain or the First Lieutenant," Sales said emphatically.

Marty took a breath then asked,

"Do you have the clothes in store?"

"Yes, but as I said it's only for the captain or First Lieutenant to order that."

Marty walked away before he said something he would regret.

On his way to the wardroom, he met Smethers, the third lieutenant, on his way up to take the watch. He knew he wouldn't see the first as he always locked himself away in his cabin when he was off watch. He did, however, have to pass his door on his way to the wardroom.

As he got closer, he became aware of a strange smell. It was pungent and sweet, and it seemed to be coming from the First Lieutenants cabin. Puzzled, he went into the wardroom and wrote up his lists into a form that could be entered into the ship's books.

They were sailing up past the Northeast corner of Scotland and the temperature had noticeably dropped. The first stubbornly refused to have extra clothes issued.

Marty searched out Tom while he was off duty and found him splicing a broken piece of the fore mast rigging. So, on the pretext of monitoring his work he took the chance to get a report on the conditions below.

It was worse than he feared, the men were suffering badly. There were four men who should be being looked after by the surgeon in the brig awaiting punishment by flogging for being unable to work because of the cold. He thought about the first who didn't seem to notice the cold at all and thought that strange. He had read the punishment book and knew that there had been regular beatings with excessive amounts of lashes. Mainly for minor infractions that should have been handled by denial of privileges.

"Tom, I've noticed an odd smell around the first's cabin when he is off duty. Could you find an excuse to pass by and see if you recognise it?"

"Aye, I will wander down when he is off watch tonight. I will use the excuse that you asked for me if I is stopped."

"Perfect. Let me know what you think as soon as you can."

As it turned out, a storm hit that evening and they didn't get a chance to check out the smell as all hands were needed to manage the ship. But the next morning dawned bright and clear and Marty had the watch. The first, as usual was nowhere to be seen.

Tom came up from below carrying Marty's heavier pea coat and climbed up the steps to the quarterdeck. He helped Marty out of the mid-weight overcoat he was wearing and helped him on with the pea coat. As he held it for Marty to put his arms in, he whispered,

"It be opium, I smelt it when I were in India with the Falcon back in '92. He be smoking it."

Marty had read something about opium smokers and how they could become addicted. He had a vague recollection that if they had their supply cut off, the outcome wasn't good.

"Have Matai meet me by the bread room when the first is next on watch at four bells."

The first lieutenant's cabin, apart from the captain's, was the only one with a lock on the door. But that didn't even slow him down. Marty had it unlocked in a couple of seconds as the lock wasn't worth the metal it was made of. Matai was positioned to see the approaches to the cabin as look out.

He searched his sea chest (also locked) and found a large package with a couple of pounds of a soft, dark brown resin which Marty could smell was Opium.

There wasn't more anywhere else, just a couple of long pipes. So, he left the cabin as he found it, locking the chest and door on his way out. Marty took the package into the wardroom and making sure the third was asleep, opened the gun port and dumped it in the sea.

He then went to bed and waited.

At fifteen minutes after midnight, he heard the first come down and unlock his cabin door. Thirty minutes later, there was a howl and banging as if things were being thrown around. The door to his cabin burst open and the first stood in it with a pistol in his hand. His eyes were wild, and he was wearing little more than a pair of breeches.

"WHERE IS IT?" He screamed at him waiving the pistol around. Marty didn't answer just looked at him with as good an approximation of astonishment as he could muster.

"WHERE – IS – IT?" He screamed again, and this time pointed the gun straight at Marty's chest.

"I'm sorry, sir, you have me at a disadvantage," Marty squawked in mock fright. "What are you looking for?"

The first got himself under control with a visible effort and said,

"I want this ship searched from top to bottom," he said, "I want my package found."

"Aahh. What are we looking for?" Marty enquired.

"Just bring me every package you find!" The first ordered shrilly.

Marty and the third hauled all the midshipmen out of bed and put them to searching every chest, satchel, sea bag and hammock. They were very thorough. Marty insisted on it. It was dawn before they finished and by then the first was found curled up in a ball shivering and sweating at the same time.

Marty had Tom help him to his cabin. By mid-day, he was in a very bad way. He appeared on deck and went from person to person asking

"Where is it? Give me a little bit if you have it. Just a little bit."

Then he screamed and ordered the men to be flogged for disobeying him.

Marty looked across the deck at Tom, who nodded. He walked up to the first and whispered something in his ear. The first went almost rigid and looked at Marty in horror his eyes wide. His mouth opened and closed, and Marty whispered again.

Just then, the captain came on deck and stood watching the scene before him with all the fascination of a rabbit in front of a stoat.

Marty whispered something else and looked across at the captain.

Jonny took a staggering step away from Marty and pushed him away with a hand to his chest. He pointed at the captain and stepped towards him. His face twisted in agony as he let out a howl then reached out and took up a marlin spike.

"You – You fucking asshole! What have you done with my stuff?"

"Your stuff? Your stuff? What are you talking about Jonny?" Said a completely surprised Captain.

"Jonny? Jonny! My fucking name is Jonathon, you deluded piece of shit. Now give me my stuff or I will beat your brains out!"

That was what Marty was waiting for. He pulled a pistol from his coat pocket and said,

"Mr. Phillips, you have threatened the Captain in front of witnesses. I must ask you to put the spike down and allow yourself to be placed under arrest."

He cocked the pistol with a loud click to make his point.

Phillips stopped and turned around, looking at all the men who were now watching the drama unfold. He turned in a circle looking at all the faces once then twice. Then looked at Marty who had his killers face on.

He dropped the spike and, with his eyes fixed on the horizon, walked over to the rail. without looking back he climbed over the side. Marty made no attempt to rescue him or call man overboard.

There was silence for several seconds after the splash and then the men started to cheer.

"SILENCE ON THE SHIP!" Marty roared.

Gradually, the cheering died down. Marty looked around then walked over to the Captain.

"Are you unhurt, sir?" He asked

"What? What? I am fine. What just happened?"

"The first lieutenant had some kind of fit," Marty lied.

"Oh, poor Jonny. He took his duties so seriously it must have gotten to him," the Captain said sadly, but then beamed at Marty. "But every cloud has a silver lining! You can be my first now!"

The Captain walked to the front of the quarterdeck and announced in a loud-ish voice.

"Ya hear, there? Lord Candor is now the first lieutenant." That elicited another round of cheering.

Marty saw the Captain back to his cabin with a promise to visit him later for tea and then went on deck and asked Tom to get the purser. He ordered a mid to gather all the officers and warrants on the quarterdeck.

When they were all there, he addressed the purser first.

"Mr. Sales, you will issue every man with extra clothing and the wherewithal to make gloves and scarves if they ask."

Sales looked like he was going to say something but took one look at Marty's face, spun on his heel and went below.

"Master at arms! Release the men in the brig and have them report to the surgeon. If he isn't sober enough to treat them get him on deck and sober him up by whatever means necessary."

He looked the others over.

"From now on, you will not use starters on the men. Nor will they be forbidden to laugh or talk. If I catch anyone abusing any crewmen or ship's boys, they will take a turn at the grating." He looked around their faces, noting which ones weren't happy.

"Do I make myself clear?" he asked.

They all nodded or said aye, aye.

"Mr. Smethers is the new second and Franklin is acting third. Peters?"

"Aye aye, sir?" said the oldest mid. "You are now senior mid, and we will resume your educations as I believe they have been sadly neglected."

He dismissed them.

Tom and the boys appeared.

"And what can I do for all of you?" Marty asked.

"Oh, we was just wondering if you wanted us to pitch the Captain over the side for you," John laughed.

Wilson flexed his huge arms and grinned at him.

"He is harmless and living in his own little world. It was the first that was the real problem. However, I want you lot to keep your eyes and ears open. There are some on this ship who did well from the old regime, and they won't like me taking over. Now you slackers get back to whatever you are supposed to be doing."

Marty looked around the quarterdeck, then up at the rigging. Satisfied he handed the watch over to the new second.

He had the old first's cabin completely removed and rebuilt with fresh timber and canvas. He also had a new cot built. It was the only way to get rid of the smell of the opium. While the carpenter and his mates were busy with that he sat in the wardroom and wrote a report for Lord Hood.

He had tea with the captain every day and dined with him when invited. He slowly and gently put the idea in to his head that he needed to be back on land to help rule the people.

They reached Shetland and ran into the harbour at Lerwick. Their orders stated they were to stay three days and to visit the local Laird. He, however, proved to be elusive and they could only send messages.

Marty went ashore with his boys, and they took a walk to Fort Charlotte. There they met a Captain of Infantry who had no more than an extended platoon of men. There was also a platoon of artillery as well but the highest rank officer they could find was an ensign, the commander was apparently off on a hunting trip across the island somewhere. Marty asked if he was with the Laird and was told he was.

*Well, that explains it,* he thought.


They were preparing to leave on day three when they saw a group of horsemen appear on the docks. The horses were steaming in the cold air as if they had been ridden hard. One rider stood in his stirrups and waved his hat at them.

Marty sent over a boat, with the third in it, to see what they wanted. The boat returned with two of the horsemen in the back. On a hunch, Marty ordered the side to be manned.

The two men came aboard, climbing the side slowly and carefully as they wore heavy coats that impeded their movements. The Marine's stamped to attention and the bosuns calls shrilled out, scaring the seagulls.

Marty stepped forward, greeted them, and introduced himself. The older of the two men, a ruddy faced man, of about five-feet-four inches with the look of a country squire, introduced himself as Iain McFarlain, Laird of Shetland. The other was taller and had ears that stuck out so far, he looked like a Toby jug. He was Captain Bridges, Royal Artillery.

"Is Lord Candor available?" asked the Laird, looking around.

Marty glared at a mid, who was openly grinning, wiping the smile off his face.

The third lieutenant, who had just joined them from the boat, leaned forward and said,

"You are talking to him, sir." And nodded towards Marty.

Both men looked surprised.

"My apologies, sir. We just received a message yesterday that you were on the island. Lord Hood warned us you were coming but we didn't know when. We got here as fast as we could," Captain Bridges supplied.

So, the old fox expected me to be Captain by now, did he? Marty thought.

"I am sure he did." Marty said with only a hint of a snarl.

"Mr. Davage, please give the Captain our compliments. Tell him that we have guests, and we will be joining him shortly," Marty said to a young mid with a runny nose.

Marty then led the men around the ship giving them an abbreviated tour. He kept an eye on the quarterdeck and soon spotted the captain's steward who nodded to him.

"I believe the Captain is ready to receive visitors," he said and started leading them towards the stern. "I must warn you that he has some individual peculiarities. Please humour him as this will be his last voyage."

The men muttered their agreement but looked slightly concerned as they went down the stairs. The liveried marine at the door stood to attention and looked embarrassed as he made the announcement and opened the door.

The Captain's cabin was, as usual, beautifully decorated and there was a table set up with a light buffet.

The man himself was splendid in a uniform richly embellished with gold and lace. Shiny shoes with golden buckles and his make up just perfect.

The Laird had a sudden coughing fit as he saw him for the first time and Captain Bridges assumed a parade ground, blank expression.

Marty allowed them both a few moments to compose themselves and then introduced them. He avoided calling the Captain 'Your Highness' but he didn't seem to notice.

They all made themselves comfortable and the steward came in followed by another man with glasses and a couple of bottles of white wine.

Marty looked at the second man and raised his eyebrows. Antton grinned back at him as he pulled a cork.

The talk was small and inconsequential and the food very nice. Several bottles of wine were drunk, and Marty finally said.

"My apologies, gentlemen, but we need to making sail in around an hour to catch the tide."

"Of course, we mustn't delay your departure. You must all be ready to see home again," replied the Laird a tad too quickly.

There were extended and florid farewells, and Marty finally got them on deck where he ordered the boat brought around and manned.

Looking around to see if anyone could overhear, the Laird said,

"Hood said we were to give you any assistance that we could. He was anticipating trouble. Do you need anything?"

"Thank you for the offer," Marty replied. "But the cause of the problem was eliminated some days ago."

Four days after their return to Portsmouth, Captain Carruthers was met at the dock by an entourage of liveried retainers and he along with his belongings left the Sunderland for good. Marty stayed for another day until the replacement captain arrived and read himself in. A new first lieutenant came aboard, and Marty and his men went ashore.

Admiral Hood was waiting at the George to get Marty's report.

"Well, my boy, you seem to have successfully solved the 'problem' but I am surprised to see Carruthers still standing," he said in greeting.

"He wasn't the real problem. He is actually quite harmless, just deluded," Marty replied sadly.

Hood looked at him quizzically.

"He was convinced he was the Prince Regent. He was always talking about fashion and his subjects. He knew he was on a ship, and he knew he was the ruler, but he had no idea what to do. So, he relied on the first."

"And he was the real problem?"

"Yes. He was an opium addict and tartar. Didn't care a jot for the crew and had built up a cadre of followers who enjoyed bullying the men."

"How did you stop him?"

"I cut off his supply of opium. He went crazy when he couldn't get any and ended up attacking the Captain. That gave me the excuse to arrest him, but he chose to jump overboard. I was so concerned about the safety of the Captain, I clean forgot to turn the ship around to look for him. After that, I just had to persuade the captain that he was needed on shore."

"Yes, after I got your message, we arranged for him to be sequestered in his house in Guildford with a guard dressed as footmen. He will live out his life with his illusion undisturbed."


A coach was waiting, and they set off back to Cheshire. They would make it in time for Christmas.

# Chapter 17: A Passage to India

Christmas 1799 in Cheshire was the best he had ever had. The house was decorated with pine boughs and holly wreaths. Caroline had fetched all his family from Dorset as a surprise, and they threw a huge celebratory party for all the estate workers and tenants.

Armand came up from Kent and announced he was to get married to Susie, the innkeeper's daughter, in Deal. He asked them if they would attend and Marty if he would be his best man.

Linette was back in France and keeping an eye on Napoleon. Caroline teased him that they were keeping his other woman away from her. Marty wasn't sure if she was joking or not.

Everybody went home after twelfth night.

Marty sent a letter to his bank and asked them if they knew an agent who could find him an estate in Dorset. He wanted to set his family up and, having talked to his brothers, farms were the preferred option. He would own them and, on his death, his brothers or their descendants would inherit them.

He turned his attention to the Estate. He was becoming convinced that the new farming methods he had read about would revolutionise the production of food and therefore the profit to the tenants.

Crop rotation and cooperation between tenants to make bigger areas of land that could be managed were at the core. Along with the proper use of manure and other soil enhancers he figured he could double the yield at least.

On a map, he broke the estate up into fifty-acre areas then adjusted so he didn't cut tenancies in half. Then, with the estate manager, he called in the tenants in each area in turn and explained what they were going to do and why. Some didn't like it, others embraced it willingly. The next five years would tell if he was right.

They lived in bliss undisturbed by the Navy until the week after his birthday. Then the dreaded package arrived.

He sat in his study and read it. General Gerald Lake (First Viscount Lake) was taking over as Commander-and-Chief of India, and Marty was ordered to go to India with him.

There was discontent amongst some of the native rulers, which was being aggravated by French agents. Marty was to find the agents, who were so mobile they might be travelling by ship and put a stop to them.

He would be given the use of one the Honourable East India Company Marine's sloops. The Marine were a private Navy and used to guard the Company ships in Indian waters.

There had to be a price attached to the half price shares he had bought. The Company very rarely gave with one hand without taking something with the other.

He was to join a Company ship called the Hindostan. A typical East Indiaman he guessed. There were berths for 6 men to go with him as well. *There's a surprise*, he thought with more than a hint of sarcasm.

This wouldn't be a short trip; he could be gone for up to three years. "Oh well, I better go tell Caroline," he thought sadly.

"What do you mean I can't go with you?" Caroline said in a voice that was full of warning and danger. She was stood in front of him and leaned over him as he sat in the chair he had pulled up to break the news.

"It is India. It's too dangerous," Martin started to say. All he managed was, "It's India…"

"And don't you tell me it's too dangerous," she snapped, "I know all about the dangers of fever and the rest, and I don't give a damn. Beth and I are coming with you."

Marty tried a different tack.

"Who will look after the estate?"

"Farrel Mountjoy is more than capable. You have put the five-year plan in place, and he can see it through. The bank and your agent can take care of the land purchases in Dorset."

Blaez came and laid his chest on Marty's lap, trying in his own way to calm his people down. Marty absently stroked his head. He had run out of arguments and knew that forbidding Caroline wouldn't get him anywhere. He sighed.

"I will write to the Company telling them we will both be going and asking them to find us a house," he conceded.

"Mary will be coming as well," Caroline added. "Beth needs her as much as me, and we will need some staff."

"Alright," he sighed knowing when he had been thoroughly defeated.

The Hindostan was a large Company liner. She carried thirty twelve-pounders on a single gun deck and looked to be about one hundred and eighty feet long and around forty across the beam.

When they boarded, they were greeted as Lord and Lady Candor and were shown to a small suit of cabins in the privileged area of the ship. Marty was amazed at the amount of room they had as it was easily ten times the area he had on the Snipe. Caroline took it in her stride and supervised the unloading of her numerous chests.

They had brought only four servants; the nurse, a footman, cook, and maid of all works. Looking at other families who were boarding at the same time, they had been frugal.

One of the things Caroline had commissioned for Marty's birthday was a chest that had been designed to be a mobile armoury. It was made of oak, had steel bands reinforcing it, two mortice locks and a padlock. It was covered in leather and looked quite normal. That is, until you tried to pick it up as it weighed over a hundredweight when it was full.

Inside were the pistols and knives that he usually carried. He had added two William-Parker-made, double barrelled, ten-gauge shotguns, and his pride and joy, which was a very rare, Durs-Egg-designed, breach loading, rifled, cavalry carbine. It was a bit high maintenance but was lighter and faster to load than the Baker rifle and about 6 inches shorter. It had been trialled by the Army a few years earlier and been rejected as too complex to maintain. A few had found their way onto private hands. He had removed the spear bayonet and saddle ring to lighten it and with practise could get six shots a minute out of it.

Mary the nurse and baby Bethany were in the smaller of the two bedrooms. Blaez had made his way in there the instant that Bethany's cot was in place and took up position between the cot and the door. Marty and Caroline had a state room and there was a separate sitting room where they could entertain. Meals were either in a common dining room, which they shared with the other high-end passengers, or they could eat and entertain in their suite. The other servants slept separately in two cabins a deck down.

They sailed in convoy with two other Indiamen, the Chichester and the Earl Talbot, the Navy Brig Sloop Victor and the thirty-six-gun Frigate HMS Doris.

The Victor sailed first in line with the Hindostan, Earl Talbot and Chichester in line astern. The Doris stayed to windward to be able to lend assistance if they were attacked. The Captain of the Hindostan, George Millet was acting as Commodore.

Marty left Caroline to unpack and went up on deck. It was strange to be a passenger and not have any active role in running the ship. There was a crew of around one hundred and he was immediately struck by the difference in the way the ship was run.

They didn't have a fiddler to make the beat for the heave but instead the men sang a shanty and hauled on the beat. They were raising and sheeting in sails and sang.

When I was a little lad
And so my mother told me,
Way, haul away, we'll haul away Joe,
That if I did not kiss a gal
My lips would grow all moldy,
Way, haul away, we'll haul away Joe.

*Way, haul away, we'll haul for better weather,*
*Way, haul away, we'll haul away Joe.*

King Louis was the King of France
Before the Revolution,
Way, haul away, we'll haul away Joe,
King Louis got his head cut off
Which spoiled his constitution.
Way, haul away, we'll haul away Joe.

*Way, haul away, we'll haul for better weather,*
*Way, haul away, we'll haul away Joe.*

Oh, the cook is in the galley
Making duff so handy
Way, haul away, we'll haul away Joe,
And the captain's in his cabin
Drinkin' wine and brandy
Way, haul away, we'll haul away Joe.

*Way, haul away, we'll haul for better weather,*
*Way, haul away, we'll haul away Joe.*

He found himself humming along and tapping his foot. Tom and the boys had come on deck and watched the company men working.

"I can watch this all day," quipped Wilson, making everyone laugh.

"Mind you 'avin nuffin to do for five month is gonna get mighty boring," added John Smith.

"It's alright, the boss will think o' summit," smirked Tom looking at Marty.

The convoy started out well but soon the gaps between the ships opened like Navy ships never would. "It's going to be a long five months for the Captain of the Doris," Marty thought as he heard a gun and saw flags flying up her masts. "This will be like herding cats."

Then in the evening as the sun set, the company ships reduced sail so they came to virtual stop! They just about maintained headway.

Boats started to run between the ships carrying passengers visiting for dinner. Everyone had to 'dress for dinner'. He put on a fashionable suit of a tailed dark blue jacket with a white frilled shirt and white double-breasted waistcoat. He chose a cravat. Caroline took it away and replaced it with another that matched his suit.

They entered the dining area and were handed a glass of champagne by stewards. They circulated meeting the other passengers and making small talk.

They met General Lake, and he intimated that he would like to have some time for a 'chat' at some point but then introduced them to his wife, Nikola. She was tiny, probably no more than four-feet-eleven. She had a mane of red hair, hazel eyes and a wicked grin. She was probably around forty years old but had an energy that belied that.

Caroline took to her immediately, and they were soon chatting intimately and giggling over observations about the other passengers.

Marty and the General stood together and scanned the room. There stood Mr. and Mrs. Templeton-Booth. He was a London-based banker on his way to India to set up a branch in Madras. He was dressed in a bland, last year's fashion, suit and she was in a pink creation that looked like it was made by a confectioner rather than a dress maker.

Near them was another military man, Colonel Masters, in the uniform of the Bengal Army. He was alone and looking as if he was working up the courage to approach the General and Marty.

There were two couples in a huddle, laughing and chatting, who were the Forbes and Goldsmiths. Both Senior Controllers on their way out to take over departments of the Company.

The last couple was an Indian and his wife. Ranjit Sihng. A giant of a man. At six-feet-four-inches in his bare feet he had to be very careful of the deck beams. He wore a turban with a jewel set in the middle and sported a neatly trimmed beard and handlebar moustache. His suit was made of silk of a pale cream and the buttons were gold inset with diamonds. He had a ceremonial dagger at his waist and wore iron jewellery that Marty noted could probably be used as weapons as well. His wife kept herself to herself and watched the other passengers with intelligent eyes.

"He is a Sikh," the general informed him. "More accurately a Nihang, one of the warrior classes. He is of high rank and touchy of his honour. Other than that, a thoroughly nice chap. Speaks excellent English."

Sihng made his way over to them and bowed,

"Lord Candor, I presume. General," he said in a baritone voice.

"Good evening, Mr. Sihng," Marty said.

Sihng had already recognized a fellow warrior in the young man in front of him and his trained eye had spotted the slight bulge caused by the fighting knife which was in its usual place on the back of his belt.

"I understand you are also a lieutenant in His Majesty's Navy," Sihng stated.

"Why yes, I have the honour to serve. You are well informed, sir."

"I make it a point to know who I am travelling with." He smiled back.

The gong for dinner was struck, and they all took their places.

The next day, Marty felt in need of exercise, so he found Matai and asked him to practice knife fighting with him. They found an empty spot on the fore deck and faced off. The two were so accomplished they used bare steel.

The rest of Marty's boys gathered to watch with Caroline, who held Beth in her arms. Blaez laid at her feet.

The clash of steel soon attracted quite an audience and there were soon cries of astonishment and admiration as the two men's blades moved in a blur of speed. Marty finally got the upper hand as Matai made the tiniest of mistakes and found himself with Marty's blade at his throat.

Both men were sweating and grinning as they disengaged. Marty looked around and saw Sihng in the crowd, who looked him in the eyes, clapped his hands, and bowed slightly. Marty walked over to him as he put his blade back in its sheath.

"You are an exceptional knife fighter, my Lord," he observed wryly, "Do they teach that to officers in the British Navy?"

"Not the officers," Marty replied

Sihng raised his eyebrow at that and cocked his head slightly to one side.

"I came up from the ranks."

"Oh, I didn't know."

"Why should you. My past isn't public knowledge. Do you want to join me and my men at weapons practice?"

Sihng looked surprised then nodded.

"I would be honoured to. Do you practice every day?"

"We try to. It pays to be honed in our profession, doesn't it?"

"I will change into something more suitable and join you directly," Sihng said as he turned away.

Marty had the boys pair up for sword drill next and found that several passengers were asking if they could join in. Marty was organizing pairings when Sihng returned. He was dressed in a blue coat that was longer at the back than the front, white, baggy, knee-length trousers, and a conical turban with a trident mounted on it. He wore his knife and a straight bladed sword.

"Are you rested?" He asked Marty.

Marty grinned and replied,

"You want to fence?"

"I doubt you fence." Sign grinned back.

"Well, you are a site bigger than me, but I'll give yer a go." Marty laughed.

Marty drew his hanger and Sihng his Khanda. Marty evaluated it in a glance. The blade was broader at the point than the hilt and the point was blunt, both edges were sharp, and one side had a strengthening plate along most of its length. The hilt had a large plate and finger guard connected to the pommel, which was round and flat with a spike projecting from its centre.

Marty was also evaluating Sihng. He had extraordinary reach due to his height. He looked balanced in his stance with his weight evenly spread and knees bent. He held his sword upright with his left hand flat against the blade. His eyes were fixed on Marty's.

Marty held his sword low and circled to his left.

Sihng matched him.

Marty feigned an attack from low to high.

Sihng swayed away and attacked with a wide sweep of his sword at Marty's head.

Marty ducked under it and made a backhand swing of his own, forcing him to jump back.

Sihng smiled and went back into guard position.

Marty settled again.

Sihng stamped and yelled and launched a flurry of slashing blows, which Marty parried or deflected as he waited for an opening.

There! He overextended a fraction, and Marty launched a counterattack.

Alternate high and low then a swing to his sternum.

Sihng swung away and kept spinning bringing his sword around in a spiral from above his head to…

Plant the point firmly against Marty's breastbone.

Marty sat down with a thud all the wind knocked out of him.

Sihng stepped forward, sheathing his sword, and held out his hand. Marty took it and was helped to his feet.

"You fight well, my Lord," Sihng said, "But you should expect the unexpected."

Marty looked down and said,

"So should you."

Sihng looked down and saw the fighting knife in Marty's left hand just touching his coat under his ribs.

He burst out laughing and clapped Marty on the shoulder.

"So I should! So I should! I think we can call that a draw."

Marty put the knife away and shook the big man's hand.

"Would you and Lady Candor give me the pleasure of your company at dinner tonight?" asked Sihng. "My cook is especially talented."

Marty grinned and replied,

"It would be our pleasure, my name is Martin and my wife is Caroline."

"And mine is Ranjit. Would seven thirty suit?"

"Perfectly."

"I will see you in my suite then."


"Dinner with the Indian? What do they eat? Can we eat the same food as them?" Caroline asked with concern as she put the finishing touches to her hair.

"I am sure we can, and I don't expect they eat anything that different from us," Marty replied as he tried to tie his cravat.

Caroline took over, got it in place, and pinned it with a diamond tipped silver pin.

"Do they even eat at the table like we do?"

"Well, we will find out soon, it's time to go," Marty said as he pulled on his jacket.

They left their suite and found their way to Ranjit's. Marty knocked, and the door was opened by a servant. They were bowed in. Inside the living room, a dining table and chairs had been set up and there was a wonderful smell coming from what must have been the kitchen in what, in their suit, was the second bedroom.

Ranjit was there and greeted them with a smile and a bow with his hands together over his heart like he was praying.

"Namaste!" he said to each of them then explained that it was the traditional greeting in India and translated to "I bow to you."

Marty filed that away as the first word in his new Hindi dictionary.

They were shown to the table and served a glass of dry white wine.

"An indulgence," Ranjit explained, "I developed a taste for wine during my travels around Europe. In India, we drink an alcoholic beverage made from sugar cane juice. It is more alcoholic but nowhere near as nice."

Just then, his wife, entered from the bedroom. She was beautiful, moderately tall, probably about five feet six, slender and dressed in a silk dress that was wrapped around her in an intricate style. She had gold jewellery on her hair and face with an opal drop hanging to the middle of her forehead. There was a gold chain running from her left ear to a stud in the side of her nose. She had huge brown eyes and was delicately made up.

Marty stood and Ranjit introduced her as Surinda, his wife. Looking past her to the bedroom, he could see a small face peering at them. Seeing him look, Ranjit spotted the boy and went to the door and picked him up.

"This is my son, ApaRanjit, he is four years old, and it is time for him to be in bed." With that, he went to the door and handed him over to a woman they assumed was his Nany.

The door to the kitchen opened, and the servant brought in a tray with what looked like pastries and fritters on. It was placed on the table with small bowls of different coloured condiments.

"These are little appetisers," Surinda explained in a surprisingly deep and strongly accented voice. "The triangular ones are Samosa and are pastries filled with spiced vegetables and fried. The round ones are pakoras, which are batter balls with vegetables. The last is Onion Bhaji. That is onion coated in a spiced gram batter. You can dip them in the different chutneys. She went on to describe each of the different chutneys and whether they were sweet, or sour or spicy or cooling."

Marty found them all wonderful except the lime chutney that was also very, very hot!

They chatted as they grazed and soon realized that an Indian meal was as much about chatting and getting to know each other than just eating.

They found out that Ranjit was an emissary for one of the major Maharajas who was a strong supporter of the British. He had a lot of dealings with the company and was privy to Martin's real purpose for being on this trip. He was a font of knowledge and was generous with it.

The second course arrived and was a selection of fragrant dishes of meat in rich sauces. Surinda explained what each was.

"Here we have Murgh Makhani," she said, pointing to a dish of chicken in an ochre-coloured sauce. "It is quite mild and has a lot of butter in it." The next dish looked like pieces of red roasted chicken.

"This is Tandoor chicken. It is chicken that has been marinated in yoghurt and spices and then roasted in a Tandoor oven at a very high temperature. It is difficult to make on a wooden ship and we had to make a special oven with extra layers of firebrick to protect the floor."

She went on to describe the other eight dishes on the table. Some were made of something called lentils and looked like a paste but tasted wonderful. There was rice flavoured with saffron, potato and vegetable dishes and breads. It was a feast!

They tried everything. One of the Dahl dishes was fiery, causing Marty to reach for his wine but Ranjit stopped him and passed him a glass of what looked like milk but tasted of fruit with a slightly sour taste. It was called lassi, was delicious, and damped down the fire.

After they had finished and thought they could eat no more, a tray of sweets was brought out. There were spirals of batter soaked in sugar syrup called Jilebi, balls of dough made from whey also soaked in fragrantly spiced sugar syrup called Gulab Jamun, Pistachio flavoured sweet cakes and many more.

The servants quickly cleared the table, and they sat in comfortable chairs to talk. The ladies together and the men slightly apart from them so they could talk.

"Do you have any ideas where the French might be based?" Marty asked after they had talked about the political situation for a few minutes.

"Nothing definite." Ranjit replied. "The discontent is centred in Tamil Nadu. Madras is the headquarters of the Company in that area. There are several leaders.

Oomaithurai. The younger brother of Kattabomman who led the uprising last year and was captured by the British.

Marutha Pandiyar. He and his brothers are chieftains in Sivagangai province.

And the most dangerous of them all Kerala Simham, The Lion of Kerala. That is a province to the west of Tamil Nadu.

They are getting arms and advice on modern tactics from somewhere and we believe it is the French supplying it."

"Who is on charge over there?"

"Arthur Wellesley is the Governor of Mysore, and he will take command of the joint British army and Company regiments. He is an officer making a great name for himself."

"So, I am to cut off the French supply of arms and advice."

Ranjit nodded.


The next few weeks went by slowly. Marty wasn't suited to be a passenger. He ran regular weapons training classes but felt in need of more exercise so in a moment of frustration, he challenged the ship's crew to a race to the top of each of the three masts in turn.

The captain was persuaded to agree to it and he chose four of his topmen to compete against Marty and the three Basques.

This type of entertainment was rare onboard ship, and it prompted a rash of betting amongst the passengers with some extremely large sums being laid down. Rumour had it that the general had bet the captain a thousand pounds, which was an incredible amount.

They were in the tropics when it came time for the race and with due ceremony Ranjit, as a neutral, got to flip the coin to choose which side of the mast each team would take. Marty lost, and the ship's team chose the weather side. That gave them a small advantage as the heel of the ship would give them a less steep climb.

General Lake had the honour of starting the race that would be a relay. Matai would go first and take the foremast, Antton the main, Garai the mizzen and finally Marty the main. He stood on the quarterdeck next to the captain with pistol raised. All the passengers were gathered along the rails and cheering for their favourites.

"Are you ready?" called the general.

"Aye!" the contestants roared back.

"Set!"

Bang!

Matai leapt onto the ratlines and shot upwards, and his opponent matched him step for step. Up and over the futtock shrouds hanging almost forty-five degrees out by their fingers and toes. Then up the foretopmast to the fore royal and finally to the fore truck then back to the deck by the mainstay.

As soon as their feet touched the deck, a mate blew a whistle and the next could go. Matai had created a small lead, so Antton was a couple of yards up the main by the time the crewman got started.

He focused on going up and over the futtock shrouds and was surprised when he saw the legs of his opponent level with his eyes. He upped his efforts, but the man was half monkey and reached the top a good four body lengths ahead of him. He was halfway down a stay before Antton started down. Antton did the only thing he could. He slid down the stay rather than go hand over hand.

The consequence was that he landed only two seconds behind, but his hands were burnt from the friction.

Garai shot up the mizzen mast. If anything, he was the most agile of the three. He overtook the other man by the time they got into the futtock shrouds. As they got into the mizzen topgallant shrouds, he had a length on him. As he passed him on his way down the mizzen truck, he felt a blow to the side of his head. "That bastard just kicked me," he thought as he shook his head to clear it.

By the time he recovered and got moving again, his lead was gone, and it was a straight race to the bottom via the stays.

Marty waited at the foot of the Mainmast ratlines. His opponent opposite him. He was watching Garai and saw the kick and held his breath as he regained his hold. The two men hit the deck almost at the same time and he turned to climb and saw his opponent had already left.

He set off fast but made sure he paced himself. It was a long climb and he needed to keep the pace up all the way to the top. The gap to the other man was about two body lengths and holding. Up and over the main futtock shrouds hanging by his fingers and toes at forty-five degrees. Then up the main topmast to the topgallant and the royal. He was now neck and neck. He looked at the other man who was red in the face and blowing hard.

Marty put on a sprint and reached the masthead first. He started down heading for a backstay passing the other man and watching him carefully for any kicks. He hit the backstay and started down. His opponent, in desperation, started to slide and howled in pain as his hands burnt.

Then as he was level with Marty, he let go! He fell the forty feet to the deck landing with a sickening thud. There were screams from the onlookers as Marty got to the bottom and ran to him.

He was still alive, but both his legs were broken, and Marty wasn't sure he hadn't broken his back as well. Caroline was suddenly beside him, knelt beside the stricken man and cradled his head.

"What is your name?" she asked.

"Eddings, Andrew Eddings mam," he croaked in reply.

"Someone call the surgeon!" Marty cried.

"I am here, sir," said a grey-haired man in a dark suit who knelt beside him and started an examination. He felt Eddings' legs then took a pin from his lapel and stuck it in at several points running up from his thigh to his chest. There was no response until he got to just above his sternum.

"Bring a plank," he ordered.

They gently manoeuvred him onto the plank, and his mates took him down to the Orlop.

The Captain and General had been watching the whole drama unfold from the quarterdeck. As the man was taken below, he called for everyone's attention.

"What should have been a simple contest between men has had a tragic end," he said in a voice that carried to everyone on the deck. "By the rules, the Hindostan crew forfeit the race as they didn't complete the climb."

Marty looked up and was about to say something, but the General stopped him by raising a hand.

"Our decision is that the result," he paused and cast an eye across the deck, "Will stand!"

There were cheers and groans from the passengers and crew as money changed hands.

# Chapter 18: Stormed

Marty protested that he felt that the result should have been declared void, but the two older men had stood their ground.

"We had to let the result stand," explained the General over dinner, "To void the result just because a man was hurt wouldn't have gone down at all well. We have to think of the passengers as well."

"I could have saved myself a lot of money," chipped in the captain with a wry smile, "That fall cost me a thousand pounds and a damn."

Just then, a crewman entered the dining room and made his way to the captain and whispered something to him.

"Excuse me," he apologized as he folded his napkin onto his plate. "There is bad weather building, and I am needed on deck."

He left, and Marty could feel the deck beginning to move as the sea picked up. They were in the South Atlantic, nine weeks into their journey and had been lucky with the weather so far. That, it seemed, was about to change.

Before brandy was served, the ship was beginning to roll and pitch heavily, and a crewman came and asked all passengers to return to their suites. That in itself would have been difficult with the ship's motion but as half of the passengers were drunk it became quite chaotic.

Marty got Caroline back to theirs and then went to help some of the others. He returned after an hour and gave her a wicked grin.

"Some of them are regretting the extra brandies." He laughed, "It doesn't sit well in a storm."

"I can imagine," Caroline said, looking pale and holding one hand to her stomach.

"You too?" Marty grinned as he led her into the bedroom and got her sat on the bed. He got the washbowl from the stand and put it on the pillow beside her.

"Go away!" She said wretchedly as she cast the first of her accounts.

He left her to it and went to check on Bethany and her nurse, who was bearing up better than Caroline. He then gave instructions to the maid of all works to attend her ladyship.

He pulled on a coat and went to see what was going on up in deck. The storm was building, and the wind was screeching through the rigging. Waves were crashing over the bow, and he could see that they had only got storm sails set.

"Permission to come on the quarterdeck," he shouted towards the captain, who was hanging on to a stay on the weather side.

"Granted!" he shouted back.

Marty made his way over.

"Cutting up a bit!" he grinned.

"You must be the only passenger enjoying it. How is her ladyship?"

"Casting her offerings to God the last time I saw her."

"It's going to get worse I fear, my Lord."

"Just Lieutenant Stockley, Royal Navy right now. Anything I can do to help?"

"I could use your men if that would be possible. I have lost half a dozen injured by falls and one overboard so far."

"Certainly, they will prefer to be busy. Are we in sight of the rest of the convoy?"

"Not seen them for the last couple of hours!"

Marty roused his lads, who went on deck and reported to the first mate. Wilson and Tom were assigned to the main mast, John sent to the quarterdeck to relieve the helmsman and the Basques joined the topmen. Marty was worried about Antton's hands, but he assured him they were fine.

The storm built and built and reached a peak after two days. The men were exhausted and the passengers wretched. At its height, all they could do was hang on and pray. The captain had to run before it and they were driven further south than they expected.

It finally broke and the winds started to die down. The waves dropped from enormous, to huge, to large and settled down to big smooth rollers. The temperature had plummeted.

"BERG! A POINT TO STARBOARD OFF THE BOW," cried the lookout.

"A what?" asked Caroline, who was on deck for some air, swathed in a fur coat and hat.

"Iceberg," replied Marty and walked her to where they could watch it as it passed.

It didn't disappoint as it was easily as high as their foremast and two-hundred-feet across. The ice was a cold blue and they gave it a wide berth. The captain told them later at dinner that icebergs had more ice below the surface than they did above and could rip the bottom of an unwary ship.

Then a grey shape rose out of the steely grey waters and blew a fountain of spray high into the air.

They grabbed each other and laughed in joy as the whale sounded, lifting its tail high in the air before sliding down below the surface. They saw several more and some dolphins as they turned North towards Cape Town.

Cape Town was much as he remembered it and as they came in, they could see the other ships of their convoy moored up in the bay.

The convoy stayed there to make repairs and to re-provision. They had dinner with the Admiral who was enthralled with Lady Caroline. As they left his residence, she said,

"He is a lecherous old man. He was looking at my breasts the whole meal."

"I can challenge him to a duel if you want," Marty joked.

"No, that won't be necessary, my love," she sighed at his gallant offer, "I made sure his wife noticed. I can imagine he is having a wonderful time right now." Just then, they heard a crash from an upstairs room.

"Retribution seems to have begun," Marty quipped.

They held each other close as they ran to the coach giggling all the way.

The fleet got under way for the last leg of the trip to Madras. It was the end of June, and the weather was on the turn from mid-winter. Caroline hadn't known the seasons were inverted south of the equator and tired of winter weather.

"You will be complaining you are too hot once we get to Madras," he told her.

They got hit by another winter storm as they rounded the corner and headed Northeast up the coast. This one was nowhere near as bad as the one in the South Atlantic, but it managed to scatter the convoy all the same. Marty had a strong, but private, view that merchant captains were too shy with their use of sails in bad weather and could manage much better than they did.

But they woke up one morning all alone on the ocean, miles off their planned route in spite of the efforts of the captain and crew.

Marty gathered the boys together to give them, and him, some exercise. So, they all had weapons in hand when the cry came.

"SAIL HO! TWO POINTS OFF THE LARBOARD BOW!"

Marty made his way to the quarterdeck and looked up at the captain. He was looking thoughtful then noticed Marty standing there.

"Would you join me, Lieutenant," he said.

*Interesting,* he thought at hearing his Navy rank being used.

"I have it in mind that we are going to be in for a fight." He nodded in the direction of the unidentified ship. "I suspect it will be a Brigantine from the description I have been given. There is a pirate operating in these waters who uses one."

"Where would he be based?" Marty asked as he had cleaned out Madagascar not that long before.

"The island of Réunion, I suspect. We have been blown too far East and are in his range now."

Marty went to the chart and looked at the plot and could see that they were indeed sailing North well off the East side of the island of Madagascar.

He knew a Brig was of about one hundred tons and a crew of around a hundred. They normally carried between ten and twenty cannons. It would be an even fight if the merchant captain would put one up.

"You have experience of fighting pirates have you not?" The captain asked.

Marty took that as a rhetorical question and just waited.

The captain looked slightly abashed and said,

"My experience of fighting is limited to a few fist fights in bars when I was a mate. Could I prevail on you to advise?"

*Takes a big man to admit that especially to a younger like me.*

"I could fight the ship if you sail it, sir," Marty offered, "Like I was your first on a frigate."

"Capital idea!" The captain beamed at him.

"If I may, can I ask your first mate to order the non-combatants down to the orlop deck out of harm's way?"

"Yes. Please do." And he called the mate over to speak to him.


Marty and Tom stood together and looked at the gun crews struggling to load the fifteen cannons on the larboard side.

"When was the last time they did gun drill?" Marty asked.

"Not on this trip," Tom replied.

"Do they have any experienced gunners?"

"About a dozen."

"Shit! Right, make up three good crews and load all guns. Both sides. Those crews are responsible for three guns each, guns four to twelve. The other six-gun crews are made up of the best of the rest. Load with canister over ball. Now, what the hell do they want?"

A small delegation of around twenty men stood waiting by the mainmast.

Marty waved Tom to carry on and stepped over to them.

"Gentlemen. You want to talk to me? Only we are a little busy right now."

One stepped forward and Marty recognised Colonel Masters.

"My Lord."

Marty held up his hand.

"Just Lieutenant Stockley," Marty corrected.

"Lieutenant. We are all men who are or were professional military men in the Army or Navy. We would like to offer our services in the defence of the ship."

Marty looked them over and saw the well-kept weapons and the competent way they were held.

"Thank you. I am sure we can use you. Now, if you will attend me, I will tell you what we will do."

An hour later, the Brig was close enough to see that they had run out their starboard cannon. Marty ran to the quarterdeck and talked to the captain. He looked surprised and asked a question then nodded.

Marty returned to the main deck and barked orders. The gun crews ran to the starboard side then ran out and stood by their guns.

John Smith was at the helm. Marty sacrificed him from the gun crews to have a hand he trusted at the wheel.

They steered straight at the oncoming Brig. Marty knew he would wear as soon as he committed to attack so as to bring his starboard guns to bear. He waited.

The skipper of the brig made his move. He wore to starboard coming around in a circle to end up with his starboard broadside against their closed off larboard guns. Marty waited until he was completely committed and ordered,

"Run out the larboard guns!"

Every third gun port from gun four to twelve opened and the gun ran out. The crews had been hidden by their guns. The 'crews' from the starboard guns ran across, ran out the rest of the guns and then fell back to the centreline where they picked up muskets. Marty had his Durs Egg carbine and was ready to call the shots.

The brig came around and her guns flashed. Chainshot screamed overhead. He had gone for their rigging. Marty signalled the captain, and they steered to close the gap.

The disadvantage with the weather gage, Marty thought, is that it exposes your deck.

They were two cables apart and he could see the brig's gun crews reloading.

"Fire."

The nine guns that were manned all fired together then four of the men from each of the three select crews ran to their second gun, laid them and fired, almost together. The two men left behind prepared the first gun for reloading. All the men then moved on one gun and repeated the process.

They ran back to the first gun and started all over, but by now, the crews of the other six were ready and fired again.

The result? A constant hail of shot hitting the brig's deck disrupting their loading and killing anyone who stuck their heads up. The Hindostan moved in closer. At long pistol shot, Marty ordered the musketeers to fire. They aimed at the quarterdeck, trying to hit the helmsman or the captain.

Marty took his time. He raised the carbine. Took careful aim and squeezed off his shot. He reloaded without looking to see if he had hit his target and was ready in ten seconds for his second.

The brig's Captain stood shaking his fist at them. His first shot had tugged at his coat as it passed through, narrowly missing him, and he was screaming abuse at his attackers. So, when Marty's second shot blew a hole through his chest, he had a confused expression on his face as he looked down just before hitting the deck.

His next target was the helmsman, who stood as the musket balls buzzed around him. A headshot was all he had to aim for. So, he took a breath, held it, breathed out slowly, and squeezed.

The helmsman's head exploded like one of the pumpkins he had practiced on.

The brig fell away on the wind, closing the gap even more. Marty signalled again and the captain wore ship. They swung to starboard and circled around behind the brig bringing their starboard guns into play. Marty kept up a steady fire on anyone who tried to approach the wheel keeping it unmanned.

The gun crews ran across and this time, an experienced man took a gun each. The rest of the men just concentrated on shifting the gun to their instructions. As they passed the brig's stern the guns fired one by one.

They wore once more, but the brig's crew had had enough and stood along the side waving their empty hands in surrender.

Marty led his men over to the brig to secure it. He was 'greeted' at the entry by the sight of the devastation his guns had rained down on the deck. It was covered in shot holes and bodies that had been ripped apart by the cannister. The crew looked to have had all the fight shot out of them.

He made his way carefully around with his sword in hand. He stopped when he was confronted by a man who stood in front of him and said,

"You! It's you innit!"

Marty looked at the man who was blood splattered and realised he was probably only a few years older than himself.

"Marty fucking Stockley. A fucking lieutenant."

He leaned towards Marty as if he was letting Marty see his face.

"Ya don't recognise me do ya. It was cus oh you that I was thrown off the Falcon. Remember me now?"

Recognition clicked in Marty's mind, and he said,

"Billy Smith?"

"Yeah, and now I'm gonna do for you!"

He launched himself at Marty who instinctively swayed to the side at the same time as crashing the pommel of his sword into his head. Smith hit the deck and stayed there, stunned.

Garai and Antton rushed over and grabbed Smith as he started to move. They dragged him to his feet and held him with his arms pinned behind his back.

"Put him in irons and find out what his role was on this ship. Make sure you round up all the crew that are left alive. I want all of them in irons and interrogated. I want to know everything about them, the ship, their base, and how they operated. They will all face trial for piracy once we get them to Madras."

He continued his inspection of the brig and was surprised at just how few crew had survived. The raking of her stern had killed many that had been hiding below decks to get away from the barrage of cannister shot that had rained down on the deck. The deck was red with blood and body parts. The dead lay everywhere.

He heard a shot and listened for the sounds of a fight but heard nothing apart from the groans of the wounded. What he did hear was the sound of a boat bumping up against the side.

He returned to the main deck and found the Hindostan's surgeon attending some of the wounded.

"There are more down below," Marty told him, "But very few who will live."

"I will inspect them all and the ones I can save will be moved up on deck. What will you do with the dead?"

"Throw them overboard," Marty replied.

"Without a burial service?"

"They would have cut your throat and thrown you over the side even if you survived them taking the ship. Everyone you save will hang in Madras and their bodies hung in a gibbet. They will not get a Christian burial."

"Then I'm wasting my time."

"No, you are making sure they live to get a fair trial."

"After which, they will hang."

There was another pistol shot.

"What was that?" asked the surgeon.

"A coup des grace probably," Marty replied levelly, "It's normally done with a mallet."

The surgeon looked puzzled then shocked.

"It's a mercy," Marty told him, "They are ending the suffering of those that have no chance but to die in agony."

"You do that to your captives in the Navy?"

"We do it for our friends as well," Marty said and turned away.


The next evening at dinner with the brig clearly visible through the transom windows, the Captain was telling everyone what happened.

"So, I asked Lord Candor, Lieutenant Stockley that is, to assist me as he has far more experience in Naval warfare than I," he explained, "But I couldn't believe it when he said we had to give away the weather gage. Then he explained that with us being the taller ship and the heel that the wind would give both ships, we would be firing almost directly down onto his deck. It was ingenious."

"Is it common for one crew to man three guns?" asked the General who had been one of the musketeers and had seen it all.

"It's not unknown for one crew to handle two guns when there have been a lot of casualties," Marty replied, glad to stop the captain's flow.

"I think it was the most gallant of actions!" simpered Mrs, Templeton-Booth, who was dressed in an egg blue creation this evening.

"All you men fought most bravely," she said, looking admiringly at Marty, the General, Colonel, and Ranjit Sihng. All of which had been on deck during the action. Her husband looked embarrassed as he hadn't.

"It turns out the ship was captained by a fellow known as Jerimiah Flann. An Irishman who had set himself up as some sort of pirate lord on the island of Réunion, which is incidentally owned by the French," Marty explained, "He gathered a following of miscreants and rejects from anywhere he could find them."

"Is he amongst the prisoners?" asked Mr. Forbes.

"He was killed when their quarterdeck was subject to musket fire," the General replied.

Marty kept quiet about the fact that the musketeers had not hit anything apart from the woodwork.

Caroline surreptitiously squeezed Marty's thigh under the table to reassure him this would end soon as she saw the telltail signs, he was tired.

"Your men are questioning the captives?" Mr. Goldsmith asked in a surprisingly high voice.

"Yes, we want to know as much as possible about their operation and base so we can do something about it in time," Marty replied, "The Captain's clerk is over there transcribing everything that's said."

"Are they anything to do with the revolt in Southern India?" he continued

"Not that we know of," Marty responded, wondering what they knew of his mission.

"I don't understand what the captain said about the weather gage," stated Mrs. Forbes, "It's just mumbo jumbo to me."

"When two ships are going to fight the one on the windward side, the side from which the wind is blowing, has the weather gage. It gives the advantage of being able to choose when you engage and sometimes being able to put the other ship in your lee. But the disadvantage is that your ship leans towards the other ship," said Marty, demonstrating with his hands.

"So, in this case, as we had the taller ship, and our lean was giving even more height to our guns it was better that we let the brig have the weather gage so we could shoot down onto her decks. Correct darling?" added Caroline.

Marty nodded and smiled fondly at her.

The next morning, Marty was in the living area of their suite playing with Beth. Blaez laid beside them and watched indulgently. He hardly left the infant's side except to go on deck to go to the toilet. The footman got the job of cleaning up behind him while all the others were over on the prize.

Caroline came in and sat to watch them. She was always touched by how easily he interacted with children. *But then, being one of nine would teach you something,* she thought.

Blaez suddenly sat up and growled as he looked at the door. They looked at each other, and Caroline went to a drawer in the sideboard and took out one of her pistols. Marty grinned at her as she picked up Beth and sat with her on her lap with the pistol underneath the folds of the baby gown.

Marty stood and went to the door, his left hand behind him on the hilt of his knife. He jerked it open, and a surprised crewman almost fell through the opening. Marty grabbed him by the collar and dragged him in, shutting the door behind him.

Two things almost made him laugh. The look on the man's face as he was faced with an annoyed Blaez who was stood in wolf pose with his hackles up and teeth out, and the casual pose of Caroline as she pointed the now cocked pistol at him.

Marty looked him over. He is a Lascar, as were at least half of the crew, darker skinned than Ranjit and quite short.

"I assume you speak English as you were listening at our door," Marty stated, "Now, I want to know why."

The man looked terrified but said nothing. Marty could see defiance in his eyes despite his fear.

"Blaez, come."

Blaez stepped closer to the man and growled deep in his throat.

"You know this breed of dog bites people in one of two very painful places," Marty explained conversationally, "In the armpit," which he pointed to, "and in the groin." His finger travelled down his body until it pointed at his crotch.

The man's eyes got even wider.

"Or," he drew his knife, "I can cut them off and just feed them to him. It's up to you." He smiled.

Just then, Mary walked into the room and stopped dead at the scene in front of her. She took it all in at a glance. Then with a murmured, "M'Lady" stepped over to take Beth from Caroline and went back into the nursery.

"Thomas!" Marty called, and a second later their footman came in.

"Give my regards to the captain and ask him to attend us at his earliest convenience," Marty instructed, "Oh, and tell him to bring his master at arms."

He turned his attention back to the crewman.

"Now Mr... What is your name by the way?"

"Dhawan, sahib."

"Mr. Dhawan, why were you listening at my door?"

Again, the look of defiance underneath the fear.

"Oh dear," Marty said, "You really are going to make me let Blaez here bite some parts off of you. Aren't you?"

"Blaez!" Marty commanded and pointed at his crotch.

Blaez advanced head down, teeth bared, growling.

"I was told to listen and find out what your mission in India is," Dhawan blurted out, his head rocking from side to side in distress.

"Who says I have a mission?" Marty asked. "I am here as a member of the East India Company."

"I don't know. I was just given instructions, Sahib."

"Who gave you instructions?" Caroline asked.

"Memsahib, I was given the instruction in England by a man who came on board the ship. He knew where my family lived and my wife and children's names. He said bad things would happen to them if I didn't do what he said."

Just then, there was a knock on the door and the captain walked in with his master at arms.

"Is there a problem, m'Lord?" he asked, looking at Dhawan.

Marty was thoughtful and said,

"No, I think we have an opportunity."

# Chapter 19: Sleight of Hand

They arrived in Madras to find they were the first of the convoy to arrive. They caused quite a stir with their prize and the news of what it was. The passengers disembarked and were met by carriages on the dock. Lord Candor and his wife were no exception. They were met by three carriages. One for them and two for their servants and luggage.

They were taken to a villa, or bungalow as it was called locally, on the outskirts of Georgetown in a leafy suburb. The house already had some native staff. A butler, a cook, and several girls.

The heat was oppressive at over ninety degrees, and it was humid. A typical Madras September by all accounts. The house was airy with all the windows open and had fans operated by young boys who sat outside and pulled on a string to work them.

All the beds had nets around them to keep away the biting insects that came out at night.

Caroline immediately changed into a light silk gown and got Marty into a linen suit that was more suitable than the heavy wool he had been wearing.

Their first meal was interesting to say the least. Their own cook had clashed head on with the Indian one and they ended up making separate dishes. There was a pie made of mutton and a rich red curry made of the same meat. There was rice delicately seasoned with saffron and cumin and boiled potatoes.

Beth didn't like the heat and was fractious, which worried Blaez, who growled and snapped at anyone who got near her except Mary and Caroline.

But they endured and settled in. The cooks worked out their differences and learnt about each other's cuisines. The butler learnt how Caroline wanted the house to be run.


Four days after they landed, Matai arrived on the porch after dark and stayed in the shadows away from the lamp light falling from the windows and made the call of a particular bird that was native to the mountains in the Basque homeland. Marty came out and stood in the light sipping a glass of port.

"Dhawan made contact as he was instructed and passed on the information, we gave him. We followed the man he met and found out he is a merchant based in Madras who deals in silk," Matai whispered, "We have been watching him ever since and have identified three people who we think are interesting."

Marty nodded to show he had heard and understood.

"Antton is watching the merchant, and I have followed two of the three and have their home addresses. We could do with more manpower."

Marty nodded and went back indoors then to the stables where the rest of his men were billeted. He detailed Garai and John Smith to help Matai, gave them specific instructions and they slipped out silently and disappeared into the dark.

Tom looked up from the shirt he was making from some lightweight cotton material he had gotten at the market.

"Think they will find anything?" he asked.

Marty stuck his hands in his pockets and looked out of the open door.

"Hopefully. We have made our play, and now we need to follow through the best we can."

"Well, if we have to search every French enclave, we're going to be out here for a long, long time."

"I know."

The next night, Marty was turned out of bed by his footman, Nigel. He pulled on a robe and went into the living room where were all four of his men were waiting. They looked like they had been in a bit of a fight.

"What happened?"

"We were ambushed," said John, "They must have seen us doing the last blokes house and jumped us as we were on our way back."

"Any survivors on their side?"

"No none," Matai stated.

"Any idea if they were attached to any of the men you have been following?"

"No, they were your general run of the mill thugs. I think they thought we might 'ave lifted some valewables," replied John, mangling the English language as usual.

"The bodies?"

"Chucked 'em in the river."

"The thousand-pound question. Did you find anything?"

"We wondered when you'd ask that," smirked Matai and held out his hand. The others all put sovereigns in his palm with looks of resignation.

Marty grinned and raised his eyebrows in question.

"I won the bet on how long it would take you," Matai said.

"That, I can see. Did you find anything?"

"Oh that. Yes, we did."

"John had to do his thing with a couple of sealed envelopes, but we found these."

John passed over some papers.

"Copies, I hope."

"Of course. He will never know they was opened."

Marty scanned the documents then looked up and said softly,

"Mahé, the agents are based in Mahé."

"Get Dhawan and his family moved to Calcutta and give them the new identities we agreed on with the General. We need to keep our word on that. Make sure the French agents don't see it."


Marty met General Lake and Ranjit Sihng at Fort Saint George. There was a tall man there in military uniform. He had a long face, a prominent hooked nose, dark hair and piercing brown eyes. He introduced himself as Arthur Wellesley, the governor of Seringapatam and Mysore.

The four of them sat around a large table with glasses of chilled lemonade in front of them.

"So, the agitators are based in Mahé. That makes them unreachable unless we can catch them outside of their territory," Concluded Wellesley after Marty had told them what they had found.

Marty sat back in his chair and thought about the problem. Mahé was the other side of India to Madras on the west coast. It was a long-established French colony. France and England were at peace.

"It couldn't be simpler," he said, "Ranjit, what do you think to a little trip to Seringapatam with Governor Wellesley escorting a number of the pirates that were captured on the trip over."

The General sat back and lit a cheroot.

"William said you were a bright boy when he recommended you to us. You obviously have a plan."

"Well, I have the beginnings of a plan," he admitted, slightly irked at being called a boy. "The details can be worked out later as we get more information. But right now, I need to get my team closer to Mahé and I don't need the French to know we are coming. So, we are going to sail that brig out of here and you are going to arrange for a Marine sloop to take us off when we are out of sight."

General Lane agreed and asked,

"And how would you like to be re-introduced to shore?"

"As prisoners. You will want them taken to Seringapatam to stand trial and hang as examples," Marty replied, nodding towards Wellesley.

"Won't seven prisoners stand out?" asked Wellesley.

"That's why you will take some of the prisoners from the brig as well. I will make sure none of them talk."

The next morning, Marty visited the cells in Fort Saint George where the pirates from the brig were held. He got Billy Smith brought out and he talked to him in a closed room.

"Still want to do for me?" Marty asked.

"Given half a chance but they'm gonna 'ang me first ain't they," Billy replied scornfully.

"Well, I have a proposition for you that might change that."

Billy looked suspicious but nodded for him to continue.

"I want you to be part of a group of prisoners that are going to be transferred to Seringapatam. Me and my boys will be part of it too. All you have to do is play along and make sure the others do as well. In payment, I will guarantee a pardon for all of you."

"How can a lieutenant guarantee that?"

"A lieutenant can't, but a Lord can."

"Who's that then?"

"Me."

"What? You? You ain't no Lord. You be just a miner's son from Dorset."

"That's where you are wrong," Marty reconsidered "Well, you're right about the miner's son bit, but I am Lord Candor."

"You be him? They were talking about him on the way back. Sayin' what a brilliant bloke he was to take our brig with a company ship."

Marty leant against a wall and let him talk.

"You be married then?"

Marty didn't answer. Instead, he asked,

"Will you do the deal?"

"Do I have a choice?"

"You can hang."

Billy hardly had to think about it as he really had no choice.

"Alright, I'm in."

Marty held out his hand and Billy took it reluctantly.

"One more thing. If you or any of the others fuck this up, you will all hang. Clear?"

"Yeah, I expected as much. It's clear and I expect you will do it yerself if it comes to it."

"Good, now go and get me nine volunteers."

They sailed out on the brig at the beginning of October and as planned, transferred to a marine sloop as soon as they were over the horizon.

They changed into typical pirate clothes and dirtied themselves up to the point no one would recognize them. They weren't treated kindly as they left the ship in chains. The marines playing it up for all they were worth. Wilson growled that he would teach on particular marine the true nature of pain if he ever met him again.

Thrown into a cell which already held ten men, they made themselves at home. They had no visible weapons but Wilson's extreme size and the mere rumour of their competence at street fighting kept the peace.

The next morning, they were herded out into prison wagons, simple cages on wagon beds, and set off in convoy with a brigade of cavalry led by Wellesley himself. It would take seven to eight days, depending on the weather, to make the trip.

They were let out to walk in line behind the wagons once a day and at night they were chained together and slept under blankets on the ground. They were never out from under the muskets of the escort even to go to the toilet.

Marty insisted the façade was maintained as they couldn't take the chance that someone would smell a rat before they got to Seringapatam. As it turned out, they got there in seven days as the rain held off and the roads were dry.

They crossed the bridge onto the island formed by the Northern and Southern branches of the river Kaveri. The eastern end of the island was taken up with a Fort, which had been the stronghold of Tipu Sultan until the East India Company besieged it in 1799 and killed Tipu with a hail of bullets, four of which found their mark.

Once inside the fort they were released from their shackles. Wellesley walked over and invited Martin and his men to join him in the main building.

The pirates were taken to an empty barracks and locked in under guard.

Marty and the boys were taken to rooms with baths and clean clothes.

Marty had a bath then dressed in silk shirt and loose-fitting trousers. He donned his sword that had been brought by Wellesley, then pulled on a light blue long jacket that came down to his thighs.

A servant came and informed him that dinner was served, and he followed him to the dining room. Wellesley and Ranjit were already at the table. Marty took a chair that was held out for him and had a napkin laid on his lap by an attentive servant.

"Good evening, Governor Wellesley, Ranjit," Marty greeted them.

"Good evening and please call me Arthur," replied Wellesley.

"Then please call me Martin."

The first course was served, a delicious mulligatawny soup.

"What do you plan to do next?" Ranjit asked as the bowls were cleared away.

"Well, we need to get me and the boys into Mahé, with a believable cover story."

The second course was delivered. A lightly battered, spiced, fried fish served with a salad.

"As escaped prisoners perhaps?" Arthur suggested.

"If we can contrive a suitable escape it would work," Marty conceded.

The three of them became thoughtful as they ate. Every now and then, one would go to say something then shake their heads as they realized their idea wouldn't work for some reason.

Marty turned the conversation to general matters as they finished their meal. The meat dish was chicken with onions and rice. Marty thought it was delicious.

"May I make a suggestion?" Marty asked.

The other two nodded.

"Bring my men in and let them and us throw some ideas around and see what we can come up with."

"Unconventional," observed Arthur. "Do you usually include your men in your planning?"

"It depends on how unconventional the situation is," Marty responded, "In our business the lines are a little blurred at times."

"But you are still the leader," stated Ranjit.

"Oh yes, I always have the final word, especially if we are on ship."

A servant was dispatched and ten minutes later, the men arrived. They were suitably respectful of the ranks of their hosts.

Marty explained the idea and put a large map of the island with the surrounding countryside on the now cleared dining table. He asked for suggestions.

They all studied the map for a long moment.

Mattai pointed to the west of the town and asked,

"Is the river navigable to this lake?"

"Yes, the locals fish there," Arthur answered.

"Where do they land the fish?" asked Tom.

Arthur pointed to the North shore of the river just West of the tip of the island.

"Here at Agram."

"If we want to avoid Mysore, we need to go down river to here," Marty added and pointed to an area where the river seemed to open out into a lake, "and then take this branch down to Katte Malalawadi."

"If I can have some paper and writing materials, I can make a copy of the map," John Smith volunteered.

Arthur called a servant and the necessary materials soon arrived.

"But how are you going to stage an escape?" The General asked, a little exasperated by the whole process.

"With respect, sir," said Tom, "It ain't no good planning a breakout if we cain't get away. So, we looks at the escape route first and then works backwards to that."

Marty suppressed a grin and saw Arthur had covered his mouth and was having a small coughing fit.

"So, we need to get to the boats and lift one of them. How do we get to the dock from the Fort?" Wilson asked.

"You can pick us up and carry us," joked Matai.

"An' I'd hold yer head underwater all the way across," Wilson responded.

"There is a bridge here," Antton observed, pointing to one on the Northwest corner of the island.

"That one was severely damaged during the siege. We don't trust it enough to use it," Arthur supplied.

"But can it still be crossed?" Antton persisted.

"Well yes, I suppose it could, but there are gaps and parts are still falling off," Arthur confirmed.

Marty grinned at the team who grinned in reply. All they had to do now was figure out how to get out of the fort.

"One thing about Forts is they be designed to keep people out not in," Tom observed.

"And the guards carry the keys on their belts," John chipped in.

"How do you get the keys off the guards?" asked Ranjit.

"Same way I just took your watch," said John Smith, who had brushed past Ranjit on his way to the map to check a detail for his copy.

"What?" said Ranjit, patting down his empty waistcoat. "It was attached through a buttonhole!"

John dangled the watch by its chain and gave it back.

"Nothin' to it."

"I must say your men have some unusual skills," Arthur noted a little nervously.

"Specially chosen for their unique abilities," Marty explained. "We cover all of the required skills for entering enemy premises and leaving with their secrets without leaving a trace."

"Fascinating," said Arthur thoughtfully. "There was an incident in France a few years ago where a large consignment of gold went missing under mysterious circumstances," the General recalled.

"Yeah, that were us," John confirmed without looking up from his drawing.

The three officers looked at each other and Marty could see the thought pass around them. *What are we letting loose here?"*

An hour later, they had a plan. In the beginning, Wellesley had been dubious about the whole process. It simply wasn't the way one commanded. But he had to admit that this special team had a unique way of coming up with solutions to problems and, amazingly, still deferred to Marty as the undisputed leader. He had noted how Marty let the men explore the options and deftly steered them to a conclusion. It gave him quite a lot to think about.

Two days later, the alarm was sounded as an open cell was discovered and seven prisoners were missing. A lot of shouting and running around also found a postern gate in the North wall was unlocked and left open. Squads of men scoured the countryside around the Island and searched Mysore looking for the missing men. Then a fisherman reported his boat was stolen and the search shifted to the river.

Marty and the boys rowed the rickety boat down the River Kaveri. They were looking for the branch to the south that would lead them into the tributary that came down from Katte Malalawadi. The boat only had a stern oar, so they had to scull it to make progress. That was fine while running downstream but wasn't anywhere near as efficient when travelling against the flow of the tributary.

Wilson was working hard when there was a loud crack, and the oar broke in half. The boat didn't have a spare, so they all had to grab whatever they could to get them to the shore.

They had gotten about halfway up the tributary when the oar broke and were now trudging along southwest skirting a large forest which took them further South. The land steadily rose as they swung back to the Southwest into a river valley which cut through the hills to the West. They could see a ridge of mountains ahead of them, but a track led North Northwest and they hoped it would lead them to a pass.

They had seen villages but avoided them as they were foraging enough from the rich land to eat without having to steal from the locals. There were streams that were fast flowing and fresh.

"The trouble with streams is that you didn't know who's been pissing in them," Tom pointed out.

More worrying was once it got dark, they could hear the roar of, what they assumed were, tigers. So, they decided to keep a fire lit all night. Garai came face to face with a king cobra when he went to relieve himself. His arrival in the camp with his trousers around his thighs caused a lot of amusement.

The biggest surprise was coming across a herd of wild elephants that crossed the track in front of them. A big tusker faced them as the others crossed the road and then turned disdainfully away.

The track led them around the end of the mountains, and they turned back Southwest to where they hoped they would find the coast. The whole area was heavily forested, and they were on their guard all the time.

They came to a village, and Marty asked by sign language the direction to Mahé. The bemused local pointed to a trail that led Southwest.

They followed it for three hours until they came to a small town. They walked in and saw signs of French occupation. There was a tavern with blue coated soldiers lounging around outside and, in the town square, a large building with a French flag flying over it.

Marty led them straight to the large building. There were soldiers at the door who stopped them entering and asked their business.

"We are privateers who were captured by the English. They took us to Seringapatam to hang us as an example, but we escaped. We walked here. I want to talk to the governor."

The soldier took in their appearance, the ragged clothes, dusty legs, British pistols.

"Wait here. I will ask." He left them in the care of the second guard and went into the building.

Marty was concerned about Antton. He was sweating more than the rest of them and was a little grey under his tan.

"Are you alright?" he asked him.

"I have felt better, hot and cold at the same time," he replied.

The guard came back and asked them to go inside. The foyer was cool compared with outside and there was the expected clerk sat at his desk. Marty went through the story again. The clerk wrote a note and called an Indian servant to take it to the governor.

The servant returned and passed a note back to the clerk.

"The governor will see you now. Is he alright?" he said, pointing at Antton, who was leaning against a wall and shivering violently.

"I think he has a fever," Marty replied, concerned.

"He had better stay there. I will call the doctor. The rest of you go in."

"Matai, stay with him," Marty ordered.

The rest followed the servant into a large airy office with a punkah waiving lazily back and forth. A corpulent man sat at a desk looking over some papers. He waved for them to stand in front of his desk and then made them wait while he finished.

The door opened. Another man came in. This one was slim with a sharp face. His hair was tied back in a ponytail. He was dressed in Indian-style trousers, a silk shirt and a dark coat.

*Intelligence officer if I ever saw one,* thought Marty.

"I am told that you claim to have escaped from the Fort at Seringapatam and walked here from there. I must say I find that highly improbable."

"All the same, it's true," Marty asserted, "We were taken there from Madras to be tried and hung because we were privateers."

"How were you captured?" the second man asked.

"We attacked a company ship called the Hindostan. We expected it be as incompetently defended as all company ships, but they had some Navy men onboard, and we got a real whipping. Our ship, the Tanya, didn't stand a chance. They killed almost half the crew and the rest were taken prisoner.

Then some man called Wellesley turned up with this great big Sikh, and we were picked to be taken to Seringapatam for trial as some kind of example."

"One of ours is a pick pocket and stole a set of keys from a guard. He is an Englishman, but he is now a privateer."

"A traitor!"

"No, a refugee. They were going to hang him."

The intelligence officer whispered something in the governor's ear.

"Please wait outside." He asked and Marty led them out into the hall.

Five minutes later, the 'security' man let them back in.

"It appears your account agrees with information we have received from our sources." He made some notes on a piece of paper.

"You may stay in Mahé until we can arrange transport back to Réunion. We will allocate you a house to stay in in the meantime." He reached into a drawer. "Here is some money for you to buy food."

He waved them out.

Antton and Matai were not in the foyer when they got there, and Marty asked the clerk where they had gone.

"They are at the infirmary. Go left out of here, and it's the last building on the right."

They followed the directions and found a small building next to a church. They went in to be greeted by a nun.

"I am looking for my men, they said at the townhall they had been taken here."

The nun said nothing, just led them through to the back where there were several beds. Antton was in one and Matai was sat on a chair beside him.

Antton looked terrible. He was grey, sweat beaded his face, and he was shivering. A studious man with pince nez glasses walked up and looked down at him.

"Which one of you is Martin?" he asked.

"I am."

"Your man has a bad fever. He needs Peruvian Bark, but that is very expensive. Do you have money?"

Marty looked at Antton, took a knife, and slit the stitching on the hem of his coat. He took out two gold pieces and held them up.

"Is this enough?"

The doctor took one and nodded. The gold pieces were Spanish and were part of their emergency fund, but Marty figured this was just the kind of emergency that that was for.

A voice behind them asked,

"And how come the British didn't find that?"

Marty turned and saw the slim man from the governor's office.

"We meet again Mr… " Marty replied.

"Brieu. Please answer the question."

"They took our weapons but didn't search our clothes. I always like to have an 'emergency fund' in case something goes wrong."

Brieu was obviously dubious about that but let it go for the time being.

The doctor returned with a liquid that had a faint yellow tinge to it and gave it to the nun, who sat on the bed and, lifting Antton's head onto her lap, gently fed him the liquor.

"It is an infusion of Peruvian bark in water. It is very bitter but is the most effective treatment for the fever." The doctor explained.

They left Antton in the care of the nuns and Brieu showed them to an empty house that had once been used by the army.

"We are being watched." Garai observed from the porch. "One in the window of the house opposite. Another 2 doors down to the left on the roof."

He walked back into the room, sat on his bed, and pulled off his boots. He took out the knives hidden inside and checked the edges. Satisfied, he slid them back into the sheaths.

Marty laid on his bed and thought about what they should do next. He knew that they needed to scout out the whole area, get an idea of the number of troops, and try and identify the agents that were travelling to the interior to advise the locals. He talked to the boys, telling what he needed.

Tom went for a walk. He strolled down the street and made his way down towards the sea. He stopped at the hospital to visit Antton and stayed there for a while. He left and continued down towards the beach.

There was a fish market on the dock, and he took the time to look at the catch and bought a large snapper. He walked back up the street to their house whistling a shanty he had learnt on the Hindostan as if he didn't have a care on the world.

"Two of them followed me all the way down and back. Took it in turns to lead and one even tried a front tail," he reported.

"Had some training then," Marty commented.

"But bloody useless all the same. I had them pegged as soon as I left."

"This fish is nice, but we need some rice and vegetables to go with it," Garai complained. It was his turn to cook.

*"Well, go get some!"* Marty responded and tossed him a couple of coins.

The market for vegetables was more in the middle of the town, so Garai got to explore in the opposite direction to Tom. He too reported a tail when he returned but also that he had counted twenty-three soldiers and two officers wandering around the marketplace. There was a building on the West side of the market that looked like a base of some kind as there were several French coming and going, dressed in Indian versions of European clothes.

They kept this up until Antton was released from the nun's care. He had lost weight and had a pallor to his skin. So, they fed him on mutton, as they couldn't get beef, and red wine, which they bought from the soldiers, to build up his blood.

Marty was called to the governor's office and questioned again. He gave them the same answers for the most part with slight variations, so they didn't sound as if he had learned them by rote. They also asked to look at his hands. He guessed they were checking he had sailors callouses. Luckily, he did as he often grabbed a rope to help a haul and climbed the rigging to check a sighting.

After three weeks had passed, Tom came back from one of his regular walks and reported that there was no tail. The authorities had either decided they were harmless or had better things to do. They all took walks over the next two days and none of them could spot anyone following them.

They started extending their forays around the town and into the surrounding countryside, building up their knowledge of the area. They identified the barracks, a quartermaster's warehouse, stables, and armoury. There was also a house where several of the tails that they had identified were living and another building where they seemed to congregate during the day.

October was running out when a large merchant ship arrived. It moored about one hundred yards offshore, and a small convoy of ox carts trundled passed their house.

Marty and Antton took a walk down to the fish market, which coincidently, was very near the small dock that the ships boats were pulling in and unloading on.

"Boxes, about five-feet long and eighteen inches square. We counted five hundred in all," Marty reported to the rest of the team. "Look like the right size for muskets to me."

"Casks that looked mighty heavy could be full of shot," Antton added, "And others they unloaded very carefully could be powder."

"I bet there were boxes of flints somewhere in there too," Marty pondered.

"That would be enough muskets to arm a small army assuming ten muskets per box that's…" said Tom wrinkling his brow as he tried to work it out.

"Five thousand muskets," finished Marty for him. "Exactly enough for a small army."

# Chapter 20: Every cloud . . .

Marty was frustrated.

The cargo from the ship had been taken straight to the quartermaster's warehouse, and a guard was mounted with soldiers patrolling around it day and night. They even had sentries on the roof! In fact, security was so tight that they couldn't see a way to get in at all.

The garrison was so small that all the soldiers knew each other. So, they couldn't impersonate them either. And just to complete his frustration their watchdogs were back.

Marty paced up and down their kitchen while the rest of the team sat around the table. He was trying to think of a way to get into the warehouse to blow up the arms before they were moved. But every plan he came up with ended at a dead end.

Then door opened, and Brieu walked in with half a dozen soldiers at his back.

"Gentlemen, I have good news. You are leaving." He smiled. "The ship, the one you carefully watched unload, will take you back to Réunion. I am sure that your fellow privateers will welcome you with open arms," he said with a smile that belied the lie.

He beckoned the soldiers in and commanded,

"Search them and remove their weapons."

They were searched, and their knives removed. Even the ones in their boots.

An hour later, they were climbing the side of the ship. She was a merchantman, and they were shown to their berths in one of the empty holds. Hammocks had been slung for them and a bucket provided so they could relieve themselves.

Garai, Matai and Antton had their heads together, animatedly talking about something. Something was decided and Garai stood and raised his head to the grate above them.

"Yip, Yip, Yey, Yey, Yey Aaaaahhhhh," he called.

Marty looked up, wondering what he was doing then heard.

"Yey, yey, yey Aaaaaahhhhh," from the deck above.

Garai looked down with a grin on his face.

"Help is on the way."

Marty, Tom, and John looked at each other, puzzled.

"I recognized a couple of Basques in the crew as we boarded. I just asked them to come to me, and they said they would."

"Damn, you people can have a whole conversation with that yippin' and hollerin'," Tom observed wryly.

The ship got underway soon after and was plodding along at what felt like no more than five knots. It slowed down even more at nightfall.

There was a sound from above and the hatch opened, a ladder lowered, and two men climbed down. The hold was only lit by the starlight coming through the hatch grating, and Marty could just make out that they were of similar height and build to Garai.

The five men greeted each other with hugs and a lot of whispered chat in, what Marty assumed was, Basque.

Antton turned to Marty and switching to French said,

"This is Martin. He is a Lieutenant in the British Navy and a Lord. He is our leader. We need to get back to Mahé and destroy the shipment that you brought in."

"By the time we get back, it will be too late. They move the guns tomorrow," replied one of the men.

"What are your names?" Marty asked.

"Christo."

"Franco."

"Do you know where they are being taken?"

"We heard the French saying that they would be taken to Kanchipuram to arm a new rebellion against the British."

Marty pictured the map of India he had memorized. If he had it right, Kanchipuram was in Tamil Nadu and was close to Madras. It was a religious centre for the Hindus, would be a symbolic place to start a rebellion and could threaten Madras itself.

"We need to get back, warn Wellesley and stop those guns from getting there." He said, then turned to the two sailors.

"Christo, Franco, will you join us?"

"This will hurt the French?" Christo said.

"Yes, a lot, you have my word on it,".

"Then I am in!" Confirmed Christo

*"Me too!"* Franko said.

"Then we need to get this ship to shore and get some horses." Marty said.

An hour later, the deck watch were lying on the deck neatly tied. Below decks, the off-duty crew were similarly incapacitated. Marty and his men were, once again, fully armed with their choice of edged weapons and pistols. They had found a couple of boxes of muskets, which the captain had stashed away for later sale, and helped themselves to powder and shot as well.

Marty steered for the coast hoping they could find a suitable landing place. As the sun came up, they could see a village, and they took a boat and rowed ashore. They left one or two of the crew loosely tied so they could eventually work their way free.

Once ashore, they set off inland, heading towards the hills to the east. Like before, they found a trail leading in the general direction they wanted to go so followed it. After a few hours walk they entered a pass through hills which were heavily forested.

They set up camp on the road, made a fire and gathered enough dry wood to keep it going all night. Then it started to rain, and the road turned into a muddy river. They had no choice but to move under the trees.

At dawn, it was still raining so they set out trudging west until around midday when the clouds broke, and the sun came out. Now, instead of being cold and wet, they were hot and wet as the temperature soared and the humidity with it.

The only good thing about this, Marty thought, is that heavily laden ox carts will be having an even harder time of it.

By the next morning, they hit a track which had obviously had many heavy carts on it. There were fresh ruts and the hoofprints of oxen. On the margins were the spoor of shod horses.

They knew they were getting close to the rear of the column when they found fresh, still steaming dung.

Marty quickly outlined a plan to try and get them some horses. When they passed through some trees sent Matai ahead as the fastest, then set up a trap.

They waited until they heard a shot and a minute later.

"Aye, Aye, Aye, Aye, Ayeeee!"

They readied themselves and a few seconds later saw Matai running down the road as if the devil himself were chasing him. About forty yards behind him, a squad of cavalry were hot on his heels.

For a moment, Marty thought Matai had misjudged his run and would get caught, but he put on an extra spurt and ran past them no more than ten yards ahead of his pursuers.

They hauled up a vine across the road, at chest height to a mounted man. The three leading riders ran right into it, lifted out of their saddles and crashed to the ground. The riders behind them pulled their horses up and milled about in confusion as they suddenly bunched up. A volley of musket fire brought another three off their steeds. Before the remaining four could react, they were hauled from their saddles by main strength and dispatched with knife thrusts or hatchet blows.

Marty quickly assessed the result. Eleven horses stood bunched together and were being collected by the men. One horse was on the ground its leg broken. Marty put it out of its misery with a shot behind the ear with his pistol.

They were lucky. They had the nine horses they needed. Plus, the cavalry men's carbines and swords. They mounted and set off cutting away from the road into the country to observe the column of carts and escorts from a safe distance.

Marty considered his options. He could:

Report back to Wellesley and return with a larger force. That would risk losing the column or if the column split, they would never know.

Stay with the column, try and whittle it down using hit and run tactics, and send one of the men back to Wellesley.

Try and destroy the column himself.

He didn't particularly like the first or the last. The second was probably the best option. It gave him the chance to harass the column and slow it up and for Wellesley to send him some reinforcements. If he got an opportunity to do the third, he would take it.

Having made his decision, he detailed Wilson to ride back to Seringapatam and bring what help they would offer. He was the least mobile and the worst shot, so that decision was easy. Then he set out with the rest of the men to do a detailed reconnaissance of the column and the route ahead.

By the following morning, they had a good idea of how the French were forming up. They had around thirty mounted troops plus a soldier on each of the wagons riding shotgun. Brieu was at the head of the column with another man that Matai identified as one of his tails.

When you added the cavalrymen, they had ambushed, that made two platoons of twenty. All the French soldiers were dressed in civilian clothes and when they had quickly searched the bodies of those they ambushed, they found no identification.

The road ahead passed through mainly flat, open country, but there were a couple of gullies they could use to get within musket range. Further on the track went up into a low range of hills, which would provide more opportunities. Especially with the mountain fighting skills of the Basques.

He estimated it would take three of four days for Wilson to get to Seringapatam and for Arthur to organize a mobile force and catch him up. So, he got to work.

He sent Garai and Antton out as skirmishers. They would ride ahead and get into position to fire a couple of shots at the front of column. Hopefully killing or wounding one or two people. They would then fade back into the countryside and the rest would hit the rear of the column while they were distracted.

They would try and kill the oxen or shoot the drivers. Marty hoped that if the drivers realized that they were the target they would run away when they got the chance.

The first ambush went well. Shots rang out and a cavalry man fell from his horse. A detail was dispatched to find the shooters and as soon as they were on their way Marty and the other men hit the rear of the column on horseback. They killed two troopers and one of the Oxen before retreating.

This caused the officer in charge to redeploy his troops. He mounted a rear-guard of ten cavalry and had another eight riding out on the flanks. The rest he split between the centre and the front of the column. The horse from the fallen trooper was harnessed in place of the dead ox. They found out fairly soon that wasn't a good idea. The ox didn't like the horse, and the horse wanted to move faster than the plodding pace of the ox. The driver had his hands full.

They fired shots at random intervals from any cover they could find to keep the soldiers on edge. Then left them to make camp without being disturbed.

The French formed the carts into a defensive circle for the night. Interestingly, they put the ones carrying powder in the middle. They lit several fires for cooking, and Marty could see that the drivers were separate from the French and, not only that, but the officers were also separate from the men. They had tents and their horses were picketed all in one place. The oxen were corralled and hobbled to stop them wandering. They had five men on sentry duty.

Marty sent Christo up the road a way and Garai off out to the left. He and Mattai crept as close to the perimeter as they could from behind and Antton and Franco were doing the same off to the right.

An eerie wail split the night.

"AYEEEEEE, AYA, AYE, AYE,"

It was answered by a shriek from out in the dark to the left. The guards all looked that way and men rushed out of their tents grabbing their weapons.

A scream of agony.

A shot.

Panicked soldiers started shooting randomly into the dark. The officers stood, shouting conflicting orders and then one dropped down dead with a bloody hole in his chest. The drivers were panicked and had to be herded together. The other officer and Brieu finally got the men to douse the fires.

Marty started his own. He and Mattai had crawled up to one of the carriages and set fire to it. By the time the soldiers realized it was burning, they were back in the brush and waiting for someone to silhouette themselves against the flames.

Marty took careful aim and dropped the first man that did. Mattai accounted for another.

They fell back and left the French to spend a nervous night waiting for another attack, which never came. Marty let his men rest.

The next morning, the French found the sentry that Antton and Franco had killed. He was lying spread eagled with his guts spilled out on the ground, his throat cut for good measure.

A driver died. Shot by Christo from a clump of trees thirty yards from the camp. He had waited there since before dawn and made his escape up a gully to where his horse was picketed.

The column nervously moved out. They now had four horsemen riding around the column one hundred yards out looking for, well anything.

Christo re-joined Marty and the rest as they moved ahead in a large arc to avoid being spotted. They rejoined the road about two miles ahead of the column.

It took them about fifteen minutes to drag brush and rocks across the road as a barrier. Then they moved back towards the column m and took positions one hundred and fifty yards out to either side.

As soon as the lead troops saw the barricade, they stopped, and the column pulled to a halt just behind them. The four outriders trotted their designated circuit.

One at the back of the group suddenly jerked upright in his saddle, wobbled, then fell to the ground. A knife hilt protruding from his back. His horse stopped and looked at him in surprise then wandered off to eat some dry grass. His colleagues didn't notice he was missing until one looked back.

They stopped and called to him. Three men rose out of the brush, twenty feet to the side, with levelled muskets. Shots rang out and all three tumbled from their saddles. The men disappeared back into the brush.

Nothing else happened until the afternoon as they were moving up a pass into the hills. A single figure was seen stood atop a ridge to the left of the pass. It raised a musket horizontally above its head and shrieked a war cry. Another appeared on the top of a hill to the right and answered with his own. A third and then a fourth joined them.

It was too much for the native drivers. Many of them jumped from their wagons and ran back down the road from where they had come. The French guards riding shotgun on the wagons trying to stop them.

The echoes of the war cries spooked the horses, who bucked and fought the bit. The four added to the confusion by shooting their muskets down into the pass sending ricochets whining around the men.

Then there was the mother of all explosions as one of the carts full of powder exploded. John smith had crept up to it in the confusion, opened one of the barrels and inserted a short fuse. He had made it earlier by taking a piece of cord, loosening the threads, and gently rubbing gun powder into them. He had said at the time, when asked why he was making it, that 'if there were an hopertunity to get at one o' them wagons he wanted to be away from it before it bursted.'

The next morning, Wilson, Arthur Wellesley, and Ranjit rode up the road, with a company of cavalry at their back, towards the column of smoke ahead of them. They passed small groups of Indian's heading back towards the coast and let them go. Any Europeans were chased down and captured.

The sight that greeted them in the pass was one they would talk about over dinner for quite a while. They passed a couple of carts loaded with musket boxes that were at odd angles to the road, the shafts broken and the oxen missing. Some of their cargo had spilled and the crates burst.

Just past them, was a cart that looked like someone had picked it up and tossed it in the air oxen and all. What was left of it, and them, was piled up in the middle of the road surrounded by its cargo.

In front of it was a scorched area that was quite empty and sat to the side of that, sitting around a fire eating roast ox steaks, were Marty and his men. Brieu sat miserably beside them, hands tied, and tethered to a tree.

# Epilogue

Admiral Lord Hood sat in front of a fire in the drawing room of his home with his friend and colleague William Wickham. They were each reading a report that was three months old and had arrived by fast packet. Wickham chuckled and turned a page. Hood glanced at him and smiled as he carried on reading the page he was on.

When they both finished reading, Hood called his servant and ordered coffee and brandy. They both watched the flames as they sipped, for a long moment.

"Ranjit said in his letter that the fellows they picked up were gabbling about demons and spirits," Hood observed.

"Probably those damn Basques," Wickham replied. "Have you ever heard that shriek they use to talk to each other across the mountain passes? Bloody horrifying."

"Shock and awe with a dose of terrorism. Typical Martin if I may say so," Hood added.

"That French agent provided a lot of information," Wickham added, "Probably persuaded to be forthcoming." He grinned.

"Martin has made a firm friend of Wellesley mind," Wickham commented with a smile, "Two of a kind. Downright ruthless and smart with it."

"Wellesley wants us to leave Martin there," Hood said with a frown.

"Well, he can stay there until Bonaparte gets tired of peace. Armand is running the S.O.F but at some point, we will want him back undercover. Those to Midshipmen, Campbell and Thompson, seem to be working out alright." Wickham stated.

"Yes, when the war starts again, we will face a France with Napoleon in sole charge. Damn fellow is going to pronounce himself Emperor soon enough," Hood replied grimly.

"Well, we will bring Martin back and put him in command when that happens. He will be, what, twenty-one or two by then?"

Wickham just nodded.

"More brandy?"

# Author's Note

I hope you enjoy Marty's adventures and the way he is growing as a person and a warrior. As usual, all the settings are real, and I try to keep the main background events in an accurate time frame. But, as the story comes first, I do bend history a bit here and there to make it more interesting.

One thing that is misunderstood is his early promotion to lieutenant, with so few sea years under his belt. Marty is a peasant, gifted, brilliant, and cunning, but still a peasant. His masters use him to do what an officer from a higher-class background wouldn't do. He is dispensable, even after he gets his title, because in the eyes of the hierarchy, he is still a peasant. Promoting him was their way to give him authority and the veneer of gentlemanliness so he could do what they needed.

The other social comment is that neither he nor Caroline are of Aristocratic blood so, even though they are titled, they are treated as 'new blood,' which was as bad or even worse than being 'in trade' in the eyes of the nobility.

I hope you enjoy the books in the spirit that they were written.


**And now......**

# An Excerpt from Book 4: In Dangerous Company

## Chapter 1 Madras

Marty and Caroline walked through the market in Madras enjoying the exotic and somewhat alien sights and sounds. The air was rich with the scent of exotic spices; Cumin, Coriander, Aniseed, Pepper and more, all of which would cost a king's ransom back in England. Caroline was looking at using Marty's status as a shareholder in the company to import spices to England. She would distribute them through the same network she used for the wine and brandy from the Deal boys.

Marty carried their child Bethany in his arms, as proud a young father as could be, pointing things out to her as they passed each stall in turn. Bethany in turn gurgled, giggled and sometimes gawped as things caught her eye.

An observant watcher would note that the couple were followed at a discrete distance by two dangerous looking men. An expert one would also spot another two that walked thirty feet in front of them.

Caroline stopped at a silk merchants stall and looked at a delicate blue bolt of silk.

"Oh, that would be just perfect for a gown for the Governor's ball next week." She exclaimed.

*"What does this cost?"* Marty asked the merchant in Hindi. He had been studying the local language and had learnt quite a few key phrases.

"Oh, Sahib this is the very best silk, perfect for making saris and only one anglina a yard." The merchant boasted. An anglina was a silver coin and was worth around a shilling.

"Don't think I am a fool and you can rob me." Marty replied. "I think it is worth no more than twenty cupperoon a yard." A cupperoon was a copper coin and fifty cupperoon made an anglina.

"Oh, Sahib is very wise, is blessed with a beautiful wife and a beauteous baby and surely knows that this wonderful silk is worth at least forty cupperoon a yard."

Marty was enjoying himself but a sharp nudge from Caroline's elbow brought him up short.

*"I will pay thirty and no more."* He offered splitting the difference, knowing he could have gone lower. The merchant agreed and Caroline asked for ten yards. Marty beckoned to a young Indian boy who was standing nearby watching them hopefully.

"Do you want to earn a cupperoon?"

The boy nodded vigorously, and Marty handed him the roll of silk.

They bought a number of other items and ended up with a small group of children following them carrying packages. They were led by the strutting boy who was first and had made himself the leader of their baggage train.

Back at their bungalow Caroline sent for her dressmaker. A talented Indian lady who was able to make western style clothes from silk, which was a notoriously difficult fabric to work with. They ensconced themselves in her bedroom to create the ball gown that Caroline had in her mind.

Marty in the meantime was in his study entertaining an officer of the Company Marine.

Edward Cooper Esq. was the thirty-year-old Captain of the company frigate Endeavour.

"When do we leave for Réunion?" He asked eager to complete their mission to root out and destroy the pirates that used the French held island in the Indian Ocean.

"Not until after that damned ball." Marty replied. "We should have the intelligence from the Belle by then."

The Belle was a brig that had been captured the year before. It had made the mistake of attacking the East Indiaman that carried Marty and Caroline to India. Since then she had been repaired and brought into the Marine.

Marty had been asked to come up with a plan to pacify the pirates working out of Réunion and had tasked the brig to reconnoitre the island. He hoped the Marine Captain had the guile to use the fact that the brig was a former pirate ship to get in close.

Meanwhile he had to be Lord Candor, not Lieutenant Stockley Royal Navy, and attend the Governor's ball.

As soon as Cooper left, Caroline had a servant fetch Marty for a fitting of a new suit she was having made for him. He stood impatiently as the little Indian tailor fussed over the fit of the suit which was cunningly made of lightweight material but looked like the current fashion in London. It had taken Caroline quite a while and a lot of patience to get the tailor to understand what she wanted. But they had got there in the end.

There was a childish shriek from the door and one-year-old Beth toddled in pursued by her nurse. Since she had learned to walk, she was a terror for exploring and would make her escape whenever they took their eyes off her. Mary, her nurse, was in hot pursuit and scooped her up before she managed to get into the tailor's box of scissors and pins.

"Is this really necessary?" Marty grumbled for the umpteenth time. "I thought the last fitting would do it."

"Be patient my love, you must look your absolute best. They will be looking at us and wondering how two commoners managed to end up as Baron and Baroness Candor. We will not give them an inch to work with."

The simple fact was that they didn't have an ounce of noble blood between then. Caroline had her title through an arranged marriage to the elderly and now late Lord Candor. He had died just two years after marrying her when she was just sixteen years old. She had scandalised society with a string of lovers after that until Marty fought a duel for her. They had become lovers and when she fell pregnant with Beth they had married.

The big surprise was that the monarch, George the Third, had not only blessed the marriage but confirmed Marty in the Barony and made him a Knight of the Bath as well as that was not the norm. They were admired by some but condemned by others as 'new blood'. Marty's reputation as a dualist kept the comments to the background but Caroline was sensitive to them.

Marty was tasked by Admiral Lord Hood and William Wickham to go to India and help the East India Company counter the threat posed by French sponsored rebellions and piracy. Caroline had insisted on going with him, as it was likely to be at least a three-year posting. So now he was stood there like some kind of tailor's dummy.

# Books by Christopher C Tubbs

## The Dorset Boy Series.

A Talent for Trouble

The Special Operations Flotilla

Agent Provocateur

In Dangerous Company

The Tempest

Vendetta

The Trojan Horse

La Licorne

Raider

Silverthorn

Exile

Dynasty

Empire


## The Scarlet Fox Series

Scarlett

A Kind Of Freedom

Legacy


## The Charlamagne Griffon Chronicles

Buddhas Fist

The Pharoah's Mask

Treasure of the Serpent God

See them all at:


Website: www.thedorsetboy.com

Twitter:  @ChristoherCTu3

Facebook: https://www.facebook.com/thedorsetboy/

YouTube: https://youtu.be/KCBR4ITqDi4


Published in E-Book, Paperback and Audio formats on Amazon, Audible and iTunes

Printed in Great Britain
by Amazon

53702408R00152